All Roads at Any Time

A Book of Short Stories
by
George Bathgate

Copyright © 2023 George Bathgate

A Clay and Bone Production

All rights reserved

ISBN: 979-8-3899-0120-9

"Whatever can happen at any time, can happen today"

—Seneca

ACKNOWLEDGMENTS

Thus far, for every Black Deer that has leapt out of the darkness, there has been love, friendship, serendipity and a full moon to illuminate the path to safety—and for this I am grateful.

I'd like to acknowledge my beautiful wife Cathy for her generous love, understanding and support, and my wonderful son Cameron whose presence in my life is a constant blessing. We are also grateful for my daughter-in-law Nekita's presence in our lives, and now for baby Mateo—our first grandson.

It is to Mateo that I'd like to dedicate this book.

And of course, special thanks to: the Chip Truck Driver, Billie and Dave, my Meditation Group and The Rambling Truths, Brad and Knute, Keith and da Mizzles, Elaine and the Realtor, River J., AA and Rule 62, Dr Spacey and Carbamazepine, Bill and the Carlsons, Debbie T. and the Simpletones, the brave students of the Polythechnic in Athens.

Many thanks also to Teresa Gustafson of TG Designs for her work on the cover design, and Deborah Strong for all her assistance with editing and formatting this manuscript.

And to ensure that I still get invited out for coffee, stimulating conversation and bike rides: Craig, Jon, Jack, Jim, Jordy, Kris, Pat, Judie, Bill and Stephen…if I left anybody out—I love you and will laud you in the sequel.

CONTENTS

Introduction 9

Stories

1. The Mass Murderer and the
   Old Dutch Potato Chip Truck 13
2. Searching for Shavasana 21
3. New Year's Eve, 1973—Peshwar, Pakistan 31
4. What Fresh Hell is This? 37
5. Saved by da Mizzles 43
6. "Why Don't You Just Kill Rambo?" 49
7. The Blüthner 59
8. Transient Epileptic Amnesia 65
9. "I Could Tell You Wasn't a Roughneck" 69
10. The Armed Robbery 87
11. The Coup d-Etat 93
12. No Room at the Café—A Christmas Story 105

INTRODUCTION

Well…maybe the process has gone something like this:

Cursed at birth with an inherent wanderlust and a need for unpaid creative expression (through the 'Three Noble Unpaid Pursuits'—art, music and writing) which—when followed blindly—lead to poverty and fledgling glimpses of 'The Primary Curse of Circuitous Spirituality' and its Groundhog Day-like repetitive conversations and cathartic Journaling habit ("I must write this down, it's probably important").

Chuck all of this into the Cosmic Osterizer, with a lifetime's worth of quirky experiences, self-deprecating humour, near-death transcendental alcoholism, and the advent of rapid technological change then blend until creamy. Pour this into a muffin tin and get baked for 40 minutes, and then pull out of the oven and you have a dozen hot and fresh stories which are absolutely Blog ready for consumption by the masses…on your very own precious websites—of which you are most proud.

But some people are never satisfied, no, some are restless and just don't know when to quit. It could have stopped there, perhaps it should have—except for that self-defeating unquenchable urge to see what's over the next Techno Hill, and the globe-sickening addiction to 'make more stuff'.

"I have to make more stuff…it's what I do…I'm 'a creative.'"

"But the world doesn't need more stuff…it's sick, it has gout."

"But this is art…and music…and writing…very small carbon footprint…and now there's a Pandemic and my Art Gallery is shut down…and my restless, Border Collie brain needs something to do!"

"I know…it's time for me to take it to the next level…I'll create, a Podcast!"

So, 30 or 40 Blog stories later, fifteen episodes on the Podcast, countless jam sessions, AA Meetings, group meditations, 'Spiritual Discussions,' and, with much idiosyncratic, unsaleable art piling up, one is left confronted by that one card—you know the one—the card in the greeting card rack beside the checkout at the 'Lo-Lo Cost' store, that shouts out, "Whither Next Creative Monkey?"

Epiphany. It can happen anywhere at any time.

The Black Deer jumps out late one night from the side of the road, having just exited from the dark indiscernible forest, while you are driving home from the lecture you just attended on "Harvesting Indigenous Edible Plants" at the local Agricultural Hall. You slam on your brakes and swerve instinctively, but the wide-eyed deer doesn't move, and your car skids onto the gravel of the opposing shoulder, coming to an abrupt stop before plunging into the shallow drainage ditch.

But the deer doesn't move. It stands immobile, in the middle of the road silhouetted by the silvery glow of July's Full Moon—the Full Buck Moon—watching, as you regain your composure from your heart-startling encounter. And then, unexpectedly, the fluffy melanistic ruminant saunters over to your passenger window and taps on the glass with his palmated Fallow antler rack.

Surprised and a little fearful, yet drawn in by the large, gentle, brown eyes which continue to gaze intently into the car's interior, and seem to indicate an effort to communicate, you slowly roll down your passenger window, and say,

"Hello…are you OK?" in your gentlest, wild-animal-speak voice.

And then, working its jaws back and forth, with its tongue protruding slightly and eyes bulging, the Black Deer leans closer to the passenger window, and brays, in passable English, with a voice tinged by a slight Japanese accent,

"Write your Book…idiot." And then, runs away, back into the woods.

Hmmm, maybe a little too much of the indigenous edible plants, I thought.

I backed up, off the gravel shoulder, into the correct lane, and followed the winding moonlit road back to my little cabin in the woods.

Or maybe it went something like this…

1. Gain Sobriety
2. Flee urban mayhem
3. Go to a small island
4. Open up an Art Gallery Café
5. Create art (again), start jamming (again), join meditation group (again)
6. Find the beauty, nature, healing, creativity, purpose,

community, art, music, and spirituality which had been missing in your sad and pathetic excessive life
7. Create a website—start Blogging the Gallery
8. Create a second website—start writing short stories and Blogging your Art
9. Create a third website—to celebrate your semi-dormant theatre group
10. Fire your psychiatrist
11. Oops, Global Pandemic—shut everything down
12. …except the writing, keep doing that—and maybe create a Podcast because what else are you going to do during a Pandemic? And now that you've got a squillion stories why not shove the best ones—the Pulitzer prize nominees—into a book?

Yes, it can be that easy, "How to Write a Book of Short Stories in 12 Easy Steps,"…almost as easy as receiving advice from a talking deer.

All Roads at Any Time—might not be the transformational metaphor we've all been waiting for to fix our collective problems, but I like it, and it resonates with my view of life. It's a variation on Nassim Nicholas Taleb's "Black Swan Theory" which explains:

"The disproportionate role of high-profile, hard-to-predict, and rare events that are beyond the realm of normal expectations in history, science, finance, and technology."

The "Black Deer Event"—and the signage—is a rural version of this. Perhaps urban dwellers would be better informed and more prepared if they installed "Black Swan Event" signage randomly around their cities.

The deer refer to it as the "Speeding Car Event", and it's usually more impactful on them (no pun intended…well, maybe) than the car, or its driver. Unless of course, they get clipped at the legs, fly up onto the hood and smash through the windshield at great speed—then, all bets are off.

All Roads at Any Time—12 short stories about life.

I was having a mild disagreement with my friend Jack recently (not so contentious that I removed him from my acknowledgements) about whether or not these are actually stories or memoirs, as they are primarily—ok, singularly—drawn from my life experiences. Mr.

Google was able to sort this out for us as follows: "A memoir is a true story, (using) fictional techniques, to engage the readers and to make the story more vivid." and, "memoirs tell a true story, which focuses on telling an engaging narrative." So, "Book of Short Stories" it is, Jack.

This collection shares the experiences of a young long-haired wanderer dodging mass murderers, muggings, revolutions, drug overdoses and dismemberment in the 70's, to the unexpected heroics of a New Wave dilettante in Ottawa, and young dad in Vancouver in the 80's. Eventually it navigates its way through some of the unanticipated side-effects of the long journey to sobriety, and ultimately drops you off on a sweet island of bliss and healing in the current era.

Enjoy!

PS: If you are a grammatical purist you will detect some errors. I chose to edit, proof, and publish this book myself and, although I was a writer/editor in Ottawa some years ago, my skills in this area may be a bit rusty. Also, I like to make use of ellipses and hyphens which reflect more my speaking style than grammatical excellence... and...my ADD probably disallows me from caring too much.

1

The Mass Murderer and the Old Dutch Potato Chip Truck

I was 17 and I'd been hitchhiking for 55 days—and I was coming home.

It was August 28, 1972 and my trans-Canadian adventure had taken me from Victoria, BC to Charlottetown, Prince Edward Island and back– almost. This was my last full day on the road and I was a consummate pro at the art of travelling by thumb. I'd had some close calls and near misses in the previous two months but this was the home stretch and I was confidently optimistic of making it back to Victoria by the following day—maybe even this day if all went well.

Aunt Alma was a sweetheart and offered to drive me to the highway outside of Lethbridge to begin my day, but she was prone to worry.

Ohh George....I just don't feel right leaving you out here by the side of the road...all alone," she said.

Her eyebrows furrowed, her eyes scrunched and her mouth turned down with a look of great concern.

"In the middle of nowhere."

"Don't worry Aunt Alma," I said, "I won't have to wait long...and I've got that sandwich you made me. I'll be fine."

I gave her one final hug, before grabbing my backpack, opening the car door and stepping out onto the gravel shoulder.

"Thanks for the lift Aunt Alma, I'll say hi to Mom and Dad for you! See ya!" I shouted as she pulled away.

I turned to face the oncoming traffic and stuck out my thumb.

It was a hot, dry August Monday in southern Alberta—rolling plains of grasses, scrub and crops, where my Swedish Grandparents had settled sixty years earlier to grow sugar beets. I didn't have to wait long for a ride, catching a lift in a truck with a young farmer named Dave with a pronounced stutter, who took me past Fort McLeod and Pincher Creek to the small farming town of Cowley on the edge of the Foothills.

The next lift was with a heavy equipment operator who was willing to put up with my company for the next five hours all the way to Trail, BC, where he worked. We breezed through the foothills and the Crowsnest Pass in the southern Rockies, and slipped across the BC-Alberta border into the Kootenays along Highway #3—one of the most scenic drives in BC, and a personal favorite of mine.

This was a great ride as it took me almost halfway home. I sat back and enjoyed the view, engaging in small talk with the driver, regaling him with stories from "the road".

From my experience, it usually didn't take more than an hour between rides, maybe two if there was a long line-up or you were stuck in a particularly conservative, redneck area where kids with long hair—like me—were frowned upon. As a blue-collar town with its fair share of hippie-kid bias, I expected that leaving Trail might take longer than usual, but was surprised that three hours lapsed before someone decided to stop and pick me up. Finally, some 'heads' (a counter-culture term for Hippies) stopped to give me a ride.

"We're just goin' to Christina Lake, where ya off to?" they asked.

"Heading home to Victoria so anywhere further west is great—thanks."

I threw my pack into the back seat and climbed in after it. It's about 6pm and the drive to Christina Lake is about an hour. The unexpected delay in Trail has changed my plans.

"I'll try and make it to the Okanagan tonight," I said, "maybe Osoyoos or Penticton to find a Hostel."

The driver and his friend were American draft dodgers in their 20's, living on a commune near Christina Lake. Canadian roads, communes, and hostels were full of young American men fleeing the draft and the Vietnam war during these years, and the Kootenays seemed to be a particularly popular destination.

They dropped me off at what is now known as the Tempo General Store and Gas Station shortly after 7pm in "the Village" of

Christina Lake. The spot looked like it had good hitchhiking Feng Shui—it was close to a gas station and store, with access to food and drinks and washrooms, and it was on the Village strip where cars would have to slow down and abide by the reduced speed limits.

Slower cars usually translated into more rides. I imagined that I'd be in Osoyoos by sundown in time to grab a bed and maybe a bite of food at the local hostel.

There was no shortage of traffic, it was summertime, and Hwy 3, officially known as the Crowsnest Highway, was full of holiday travelers. By 8 o'clock, as the evening light began to wane, and many cars had passed, I became slightly concerned.

"I don't like to hitchhike at night" I thought, "Things can get weird".

By 9 o'clock it was dusk and, despite striking my most pathetic and needy hitchhiking postures, I hadn't had any bites—except for the increasing number of mosquitoes which hovered incessantly around my head and bare arms. By 10 o'clock it became clear to me that something was wrong. People were certainly driving by slowly—too slowly—and looking fearfully at me through their rolled-up car windows.

"I wonder what's up, this is just as bad as Trail," I thought. I was resigning myself to hauling out my sleeping bag and finding shelter in a nearby park. "I'll give it another 15 minutes…a bed would be nice."

Then, an Old Dutch Potato Chip truck pulled over to the side of the road ahead of me. At first, I wasn't sure if this was a ride or if the driver had to deal with an emergency. He opened the door of his cab, got out, and walked towards me.

"I bet you've been stuck here for a while, haven't ya?" he asked.

"Yeah, Jesus…3 or 4 hours," I replied, as I picked up my gear. "What's goin' on?"

"Well…There's a murderer loose in this area…killed some people in a campsite…just walked in and shot 'em." "The RCMP and local police are looking for the guy…happened this afternoon…anyways, I'm driving to Kelowna so I can get you that far."

"No wonder it's been such a shitty day for hitchhiking," I replied, "I was stuck in Trail for 3 hours this afternoon too…I appreciate the lift man, I just wanna get outta here."

Rather than admitting me into the passenger side of his cab

though, he opened the back door to the windowless compartment of the chip truck and said,

"Hop in."

The voices in William Bernard Lepine's head told him that he was chosen to save the world from a nuclear holocaust. Although he'd spent time in the East Kootenay Mental Health Unit and the Riverview Mental Hospital in Coquitlam, from whence he escaped on July 30, he hadn't exhibited any violent behavior. On this day, however, starting around 9am August 28, 1972—Lepine, armed with a 22-caliber rifle and a 30-caliber rifle, walked into an orchard outside Oliver, BC, where 16-year-old Willard Potter and 71 year old Charles Wright were working on some irrigation equipment, and shot them both—dead.

Lepine was a 27-year-old American who had worked for a time in the orchards near Summerland, and doing maintenance work for the Municipality of Creston before his slide into schizophrenia. Symptoms typically come on gradually, in young adulthood, and can include delusional thinking, hallucinations and hearing voices that do not exist. Today, Lepine's tragic internal commands dictated that he kill random innocent people to stave off Armageddon.

He put his first victim's bodies in their Land Rover and, with the keys he found in Charles Wright's pocket, drove northeast towards a campground off the Kettle Valley Road. Around 11am he discarded their bodies in the bushes off the road and entered the campground.

The Clarks and the Wilsons had been friends for a long time and liked to go camping together. The Kettle Valley Recreation Area was one of their favourite places to park their motor-homes and spend a weekend hiking, picking huckleberries, and sitting around the fire at night drinking a few beers and sharing some laughs. Around noon on this day, William Lepine entered the campsite, chatted briefly with Lester and Phyllis Clark, and Allan and Mildred Wilson, and then, left.

A short while later he returned, armed with one of his rifles. He ordered the two couples into a truck and started shooting, killing Phyllis Clark immediately, and wounding the other three.

After inflicting this horror on the unsuspecting campers, Lepine escaped in the stolen Land Rover, while Lester and Allan—bleeding profusely and in shock—placed Phyllis' body in the Clark vehicle and then followed the Wilsons 20 kilometres towards Westbridge in search of help.

After receiving critical medical care in Westbridge, the wounded survivors were able to give the Royal Canadian Mounted Police the information they needed to begin their manhunt, in which about 25 officers participated. Patrols went out, road blocks were set up, and radio stations were alerted to warn the public that an armed killer was on the loose. By 3:00 that afternoon, as I was being dropped off by the roadside in Trail, the hunt for William Lepine was moving into high gear.

And then he killed again.

How many murders does it take to stop a nuclear holocaust? As he went about his unfathomable mission, neither Lepine nor his internal voices could provide an answer. It's over when it's over, when the shooter is caught or shot.

After the campsite carnage, Lepine drove several hours north to the small village of Edgewood on the shores of the Upper Arrow Lake. It was late afternoon on a beautiful summer day at the end of August, and 57-year-old Herbert and his 56-year-old wife Nellie Thomas were enjoying life and each other's company when the young unshaven man approached. Nothing could prepare them for what was to follow. Without warning or explanation, Lepine pulled out his rifle and shot and killed them both.

After hiding their bodies nearby, he escaped in their car, drove an additional 30 miles north and shot and killed 24-year-old Thomas Pozney—who was enjoying a little quiet fishing time on the Lower Arrow Lake near Nakusp.

I was surprised that the driver of the Old Dutch Potato Chip truck was putting me in the storage compartment of the cube van—in the dark windowless space with all the merchandise—but it was a lift, and I'd been languishing by the side of the road for hours…and there was an active shooter, a murderer, on the loose.

I hopped in and he closed the door.

When the driver closed the door, every last bit of light was gone. It became absolutely, completely dark and I became blind. I had to feel my way with toes and outstretched hands, between the boxes of chips, pretzels and pepperoni sticks to a place against the wall where I could stretch out. It was a 12 x 6 x 6 box…432 Cubic feet of pungent Old Dutch product line aromas—Salt n' Vinegar, Barbeque, Sour Cream n' Onion, Cheesy Puffcorn, Ketchup Flavoured…and Original…saturated the air. Just as I was thinking that the driver wouldn't miss a couple of bags of chips, a male voice in the darkness said,

"Hey man…where ya goin'?" I didn't know that I had company in the box.

Momentarily startled by this revelation, I tried—with no success—to determine exactly where he was inside the cube…and if there were others.

"Heading back to Victoria," I replied guardedly, my thoughts turning from chips to murderers. "I didn't know there was anyone else in here…where are you goin'?" I asked.

"I'm trying to get to Penticton," he replied …pretty wild about the murderer, eh?"

He sounded young, maybe about my age and seemed amicable. I wasn't getting a strong vibe of "crazy serial killer in the dark" so our conversation turned to comparisons of our experiences on the road. He was from Winnipeg and was going to the Okanagan to pick fruit or find other work. He too had been stuck for hours this afternoon, in Salmo, before catching a lift with the Potato Chip Samaritan.

Or at least…the driver **seemed** like a real Old Dutch Potato Chip Truck driver…maybe he killed the real driver and was impersonating him, we speculated jokingly.

And then, in the middle of nowhere the truck slowed down…and stopped.

We could hear the driver get out of his cab and slam the door…there were noises and muffled voices outside. Moments later, the door flung open and two powerful flashlights beamed in, hurting our eyes, which had become accustomed to the dark.

"OK, gentlemen," said the authoritative male voice, "I'll have to ask you to get out of the truck."

We hopped out, smelling like potato chips, into a cordon of Mounties holding shotguns at the ready, near a roadblock of police cruisers with lights flashing. My initial fear that the driver was the murderer and was stopping to kill us was now replaced by the fear that the cops would search my backpack and find my small stash of marijuana and my pipe.

"I'll need to see some ID lads…no doubt you've heard that there's a murderer on the loose…we're just checking to make sure you aren't him," he said.

The roadblock had been set up at the junction with Hwy 41, which was an access route to the U.S. border, in case our fugitive decided to flee south. He was—after all—American.

This was the first time I'd seen my travelling companion, another young, long-haired denizen of the hitchhiking culture that was so popular during the late 60's and early 70's. We didn't talk much while we were being scrutinized by the cops. I found out later, he too was worried about them finding his stash of hash and two hits of mescaline. But the police had larger concerns than the contraband of teenage hippies—a second murder victim had been found and four other missing persons reports had been filed. It was bad and appeared to be getting worse, they had to find Lepine.

We were back in the windowless potato chip truck talking about the weirdness of our situation and whether or not we should do the mescaline. We decided that it might be a bad idea in the off chance that we might have to disarm a psychopath or brave another police roadblock. The driver had decided to shorten his trip to Kelowna by taking Hwy 33 through Westbridge, rather than the longer Hwy 97 route through the Okanagan. My choice was to get dropped off on the side of the road near Rock Creek around midnight—with a mass murderer on the loose—and try and get a ride to Osoyoos, or continue to Kelowna…which would put us at the hostel around 2:00 a.m. It was not a difficult choice.

We arrived at the hostel shortly before 2:00 a.m. fully expecting that it would be closed, and that we'd have to sleep outside. Luckily, two of the hostel staff were up, quite stoned and playing "Go", and they let us in. We thanked the driver for delivering us from evil and he gave us a box of Schneider's Pepperoni sticks as a parting gift which we, and our hosts eagerly devoured…think "munchies".

Epilogue:

William Lepine was caught and arrested the next morning at Galena Bay and taken to the RCMP office in Nakusp before being transferred to Nelson, bringing his murderous rampage to an end. He was ultimately tried and found "not guilty by reason of insanity" and placed in the Forensic Psychiatric Hospital in Port Coquitlam, where he remains to this day.

I made it back to Victoria the following day despite having to wait another three hours outside of Kelowna for a lift, likely "because of the fucking murderer" according to my journal. My immersion in the darkness, fear, and potato chips has not diminished my enjoyment of

Old Dutch products—my favourite is still "Original".

Nearly 30 years later, I would meet Jackie. and her sister Barbie who would both become very good friends of mine. As it so turned out, they are the granddaughters of Allan and Mildred Wilson who had been shot and wounded in the campsite in the Kettle Valley on that late August day, and who drove those desperate miles to Westbridge for help. Jackie and Barbie have attended parole hearings for the past 25 years to speak of their family's pain, and help prevent the release of William Bernard Lepine—I have been invited to attend one of these hearings and, and, if the fates allow—I will go.

2

Searching for Shavasana

It is May 22, 2013 and the rather long and arduous Goldilocks quest for a rural property will soon bear fruit. I am on a solo cycling trip through the Gulf Islands to check out lifestyles and amenities on each of the five major islands and to get a feel for the various communities residing there.

Galiano just felt a little too close to Vancouver, and, as an avid cyclist, I wasn't fond of the layout of its road system. Salt Spring Island was a little too big and too busy—rumours of traffic congestion and narrow roads made cycling sound awkward and unpleasant. Saturna—although beautiful—was too far way, sparsely populated and had few amenities. Pender Island was a contender, but, when I finally arrived on Mayne, the Fates intervened, the stars aligned, and my Goldilocks quest was over. Mayne Island felt right, it felt like home.

It almost didn't happen. The prior eight years had been a rather arduous and gruelling journey of tragedy, misfortune, alcoholism and recovery. One attempt at relocating outside of Vancouver on the Sunshine Coast in 2011, had crashed and burned, and my realization then, that I would need to gain my sobriety before embarking on this solo rural life, would prioritize a year of dedicated recovery in Vancouver, before I could recommence my search for a rural property.

Even the process of gaining sobriety would ultimately feed me an obstacle on this quest for a simpler country life. Within a month of quitting drinking, I began having seizures which would eventually be diagnosed as Transient Epileptic Amnesia. This condition prevented me from driving for a year and modified my out-of-town search greatly. Without knowing what the eventual outcome might be (I had no way of knowing if I would ever be fit to drive again) my property search was limited to places within walking or cycling distance of the ferry terminus on each island—which explains why I was on this current bike excursion. Although I loved cycling, it was suggested that I not drive until I was six months seizure free.

Bikes it is. The first thing I had to do was learn how to navigate the Vancouver Transit System with my bike. From my point of departure in Kitsilano, it's a four-part journey to get to Mayne Island. First the B-Line Bus down Broadway at 8am; transfer onto the Canada Line at Cambie; exit at Bridgeport Station to catch the 9am, # 620 Bus to Tsawwassen; in order to catch the 9:55 Queen of Nanaimo ferry on its milk run through the Gulf Islands; destination Mayne Island...a gorgeous one hour and forty-minute journey through bliss...unless there are crippling windstorms—more about this later.

Little did I know, at the time, that this would become my weekly commute for the next 7 years (and counting)!

Mayne Island is, like most of the Gulf Islands, a hilly proposition for cyclists. As a friend has observed, islands are the tops of mountains...if they were flat, they'd be reefs.

As you leave the ferry your first task is to climb a rather steep hill to exit the Terminus. My first destination was a short undulating 10-minute jaunt to "The Village" to check in at the Springwater Lodge—a 100-year-old Pub/Hotel on the waterfront in Miner's Bay. As I sped down the hill, which approaches the Village, on my trusty old Peugot, I spied a cute commercial cottage on the left-hand side of the road which, to my eye, looked like an appealing little coffee shop. I decided to pull in and grab a coffee and get my first sense of the community—as coffee shops in small villages can be wonderful locales to pick up on the gossip and learn of the goings-on of island life. As it turned out, the business was vacant...a hair salon called "Mayne Cuts" which had occupied the space for the past decade had just closed its doors within the last several months. The "For Lease" sign indicated a monthly rent of $550—cheap by Vancouver standards, and said to call Dave for further info.

Friends, who are unquestionably smarter than I, had suggested that it might be wise to rent before purchasing—to try living in the rural setting prior to buying to see if I was cut out for island life. As it turned out, this little commercial cottage which held great visual and locational appeal (stunning views, waterfront property, proximity to the village and the ferry) was also dual zoned residential—I could live in it as well as run a small business. Although my original intention was just to rent a cottage as a residence—not run a business—I found the concept unexpectedly appealing..."artist in residence" was the first thought that came to mind. Yeah. Perhaps I could use this space as a studio for my ceramic mask making and other creative projects' I had pending ...I'd have to call Dave the landlord to discuss.

At this point, I was in no hurry. I had an island to explore and the call to Dave could wait. Although Mayne felt good, I still needed to explore its nooks and crannies to determine its suitability for my needs. I checked in at the Springwater Lodge—which is the oldest continually operating Hotel in BC.—where I'd be staying on this two-day adventure. At the time, the rooms above the pub were available for $40 per night...rustic and worn, it very much felt like staying at a Youth Hostel. There was a shared bathroom/shower, and the rooms were only lockable from the inside...

"Don't worry, nothing ever gets stolen here, Mayne Islanders are very honest," Tessa the affable barmaid assured me.

As quaint as this reassurance was, years of urban conditioning had taken its toll—it involved a leap of faith to leave my "stuff" in an unlocked room. But it was charming and I loved it. The strength of the Springwater Lodge lies in its restaurant/pub and the outdoor deck, which may be the sweetest place in BC to grab a meal and watch the sun go down.

Almost everything that I saw on these initial trips to Mayne Island charmed me. Perhaps I was looking at the world through the rose-coloured glasses of those new to sobriety, but in fact, so much of what I saw and whom I encountered fed my enchantment. The Village itself is small—perhaps a collection of a dozen-plus businesses—which reflects its rather intimate yearly population of roughly 1,000 good citizens. It seemed to have everything one needs to cover the basics: 3 grocery stores, a liquor store (for those so inclined), a gas station, 3 restaurants, a gaggle of unique shops, ubiquitous realtors, and a fabulous little bakery that opened sprightly at 6am every day.

Some remaining heritage buildings from the late 1800's (The Agricultural Hall, Museum, and Springwater Lodge) give it a comforting sense of community and continuity. Other island amenities include a lending library, a Hardware Store, a Community

Centre and a second retail gathering in the middle of the island known as the Fernhill Centre. If I was going to rent the little vacant cottage/business from Dave I would become part of "The Village"...how cool is that?

Perhaps the greatest appeal of Mayne though, is its natural beauty and outdoor amenities (I would later discover that its citizens are yet another wonderful attribute, but that would come later) The Gulf Islands are a uniquely beautiful micro-climate which has been compared to the Mediterranean for its low precipitation and above average warmth.

As I cycled around this tranquil rock I encountered dense rain-forest woodlands, pastoral heritage farmland, rare stands of Garry Oak and Arbutus, and a beautiful selection of bays and beaches to toss down a blanket and make an afternoon of it. There are some fabulous parks with great hiking opportunities, a heritage photo-op lighthouse, Mt. Parke with its mesmerizing vistas, and, an unexpected treasure—the well-tended Japanese Gardens.

The fauna, are equally varied and enchanting. Deer abound—both the indigenous black-tailed, and the pernicious European fallow...and in fact, the wildlife is just too plentiful to write up in this article—so I won't try. Whether in the ocean, in the air or on land, if you choose to live on a Gulf Island you will be living "in" nature not just alongside it. Nature envelopes you in a charming and therapeutic way.

My brief Mayne Island excursion was drawing to a close as I had obligations back in Vancouver. Of the many properties, hamlets, and rural communities that I had visited over the last five years of this quest...just like Goldilocks and her porridge, this one tasted just right. I had Dave's number and would call him to find out the scoop on the vacant business.

Shortly after I returned to Vancouver, in late May of 2013, I called the landlord to find out more about the situation on Mayne, ask questions, and gather a bit of info. The building was indeed zoned commercial/residential which covered my need for accommodation on the island and gave me the possibility of opening a little business, making a little cash, and having a cool project to work on. It was a 10-acre waterfront parcel, with four additional cottages that were rented out, either long-term or for summer vacation rental.

John Collinson, one of the original settlers from the mid-1800s is buried on the property, with his first nations wife and several ill-fated children. Because Collinson was one of the original European settlers in the area, and had brought apple trees with him to start an orchard in the "New World", this property has—reputedly—the oldest apple trees in BC—making this particular piece of land significant from a heritage perspective.

Ideas for a business, although unformed as yet, were germinating. What could I do there? As I was completely bereft of skills, talents, aptitudes or business acumen my first thought was...artist studio. As I was also—at the time—completely devoid of motivation, drive, or work ethic my other embryonic idea was "self-serve coffee bar"...these two ideas would have to fall into bed together and germinate further so I could convince the landlord that I actually had a business plan, and was not just another flaky guy wanting to open up an ...Art Studio Café.

I arranged to meet Dave the landlord back on Mayne in early June for mutual reassurance.

As I re-read my Journal during the early days of this exploration I am struck by two things: my wide-eyed interpretation of simple encounters as a kind of magical projection of wonderment (a woman carrying a basket of cilantro down a dusty country road would take on almost mystical qualities) and; the ongoing internal struggle between the two halves of my psyche as I weighed the pros and cons of this decision...uncertainty vs. impulsive commitment, indecision versus strong desire—I was having a dialogue with myself on the pages of my Journal as I sorted out my internal tendency to over-think. Problems versus possibilities...I quite literally rejected the whole concept three times before I would ultimately commit. Blessedly, magic and visceral pull would eventually win out over fear and indecisiveness ...but we're not there yet.

The June 12 meeting with Dave went well. As it turned out we had worked together as young guys in the 70s, so there was a decent cordial recollection of being work chums from another era. Even this diminishes some of the misgivings and creates hints of inevitability. I managed to get inside the space, take some measurements and do some imaginings of what it might become under my tutelage.

The cottage is petite...around 600 square feet with a cool front porch and ground level rancher-style access. The windows are plentiful heritage multi-pane with tons of light and stellar site lines. The best view is of Galiano Island and Active Pass through which all of the regional ferry traffic travels. The kitchen and bathroom are small but adequate, and, as an out-of-town, part-time dwelling it works magnificently for my needs.

Its suitability as a business though, will be determined by the appropriateness of my ideas and the efficacy of "my plan"...which does not yet exist, although my Journal entries give an early indicator of "art-cycle-website-sculpture-café-thing"...I'm good at vague.

As these were my early days exploring Mayne Island, I was still in need of further convincing that this place had what I was in need of, what I was searching for—serenity and the muse.

Although Dave's commercial property had incredible appeal and seemed perfectly suited to my "vision dream" I needed to unearth the tranquility and unleash "the muse"—that almost indecipherable thing that would allow creative passions to flow.

After years of urban cacophony and living a life that had been turned up to "11" I was in serious need of chillout. The difference between Vancouver and Mayne is vast. Although they are only 30 kilometres and a short ferry ride apart, the sense of decompression one gets upon disembarking from the ferry onto this idyllic rock is immediate. Things slow down, noises abate, moments of bliss appear, and circadian rhythms tap you gently on the shoulder to remind you when it's time to eat, or whisper in your ear "lights out...time to shut 'er down for the day".

Beaches on warm summer days offer moments of sublime joy...the sounds of happy children discovering the magic of ocean-side play, while dogs run in slo-mo after tossed Frisbees, bathed in a golden light while gentle breezes blow and the tides lap. Forest trails and favourite mountain vistas can provide similar moments of serene beauty. Climbing the local peak and sourcing out a secluded spot with equal parts sun-generated warmth and the serenade of trees and birds is a fabulous way to meditate. OK....tranquility—check.

Despite my earlier indecisiveness and waffling, I knew from the moment that I saw Dave's little commercial cottage that this quirky setting would provide a perfect tableau to unleash the creative inspirations which had been bottled up inside of me for some time. Whether suppressed or dormant, they were ready to come forth. My muse needed irony and diversity, and a boatload of new and unique experiences which the Gallery—Studio—Café, and life on Mayne Island would provide in spades. What tragedy and hard drinking had squelched, sobriety, stimulus, serendipity and synchronicity let flourish. Writing the script and setting the stage for this new play, unleashed some hidden talents, and gave creative energy to new roles I would be required to perform. As a creative generalist, they would be many—finding one's Muse—check.

Despite the seeming perfection of Mayne Island and Dave's little cottage business for my needs, my indecisiveness dies hard and I needed to return to Vancouver for further pondering, worry and excessive pensive thinking. In fairness to Dave, as the weeks slipped by and I'd not come to a firm decision, I called him to remove myself as a potential candidate for occupancy…but I couldn't get the islands or the place out of my thoughts so I planned another trip in early July to do a final round-robin of my favourite island contenders… Saturna, Pender and Mayne. Unlike Goldilocks, I have to test each bowl of porridge several times.

After a year without wheels, I am seizure free and back on the road and it does feel good. Liberating. I use my van as a camper when I am on these road trips for the convenience of being able to pull over and sleep anywhere on these accommodation-challenged islands…especially in summertime. I love all of these islands, and they each have something unique to offer, but there was only one "Dave's Cottage"… and that was on Mayne.

It was on this trip that the ideas for the business were congealing and here that I first made reference to the "Shavasana* Chillout Project", and also germinated the name I would give to my mask making activities, "Clay and Bone" (clayandbone.com) My thoughts, creative energy and focus were now being absorbed by this looming commitment. It seemed there was no turning back, so, a few days later I called Dave to tell him I definitely wanted it and was ready to commit. (*Shavasana is a Sanskrit word meaning "corpse pose" and is the last position in Yoga, where you lie on your back, breathe deeply and relax—integrating your entire Yoga practice. It's also the name I chose for my new business, "Shavasana Art Gallery and Café"

Despite this, my capacity for waffling and indecision seemed boundless. I awoke the next day with serious apprehension and "buyer's remorse". Once again, I felt like bailing on the whole project

But I didn't.

I continued my decision struggle debate internally and within the pages of my Journal…"march forward …explore… evolve ..learn", I exhorted myself, and also from the Journal "this project may provide the necessary "raison d'etre" to boost creative energies and passions"… I would "need to get in the correct mind space" I told myself, so I could "experiment with the place as an incubator for: website development, writing, creative space, playground, business, and the experience of living in a small community on an island."

I obviously required a lot of convincing, which only I was capable of doing. The two halves of my Gemini brain were fighting it out. And finally, from the Journal:

"If not this, what?"

The desire to end the search and begin the creative work was strong—I called Dave to meet up on Mayne and sign the lease.

I would reject the place one last pathetic time before the ink was dry.

It was all set. I was to meet Dave back on Mayne, the August 1st long weekend to sign the lease and take possession. As some good friends happened to be vacationing there, I came over a day early to hang out with them. Dave had given me keys to the place so I could show it to Craig, Zoë, and Daniella, and also stay there for a couple of nights.

As I fumbled with the keys, getting ready to give a little tour of the new space, my soon-to-be new neighbour—Billie—came over and awkwardly injected herself into our group—acting, I suppose, as an unexpected and uninvited "tour guide." Unbeknownst to me, Billie was also the de facto caretaker, cleaning lady and security guard for the property—and also had a bunch of her stuff stored there for the interim.

She was also exhibiting—as I would eventually find out—some old fashioned "island familiarity" (not to be confused with nosiness) which we city folk were just plain unaccustomed to.

In a word—it was weird.

And of course, my dear friends, over dinner après, had to remind me of this and embellish upon it—they were British after all. "She likes you, you know"…"She'll be over all the time"…"It'll be like Kathy Bates in the movie *Misery*"…"She's going to break in and tie you to your bed" …and on, and on…..and on. All in good fun.

As I retired back to the cottage for the evening, the clouds had rolled in, the wind had picked up and there was a hint of rain—it was a dark and stormy night.

As I got ready for bed, there was a sharp rap on the front window.

"Who is it?" I quailed.

"It's me, Billie…your next-door neighbour."

With trepidation I flung open the curtains and there she was, face inches from the window, wearing a bike light on her ever-present safari hat.

"It's blowing pretty hard out tonight," she said, "sometimes we have power outages and you might need…candles!" She raised aloft a couple of candles in each hand.

As I absorbed this apparition I said,

"Uuuuh…I think I'm good Billie…I have a flashlight—thanks though!"

The Brits were right…it was going to be a nightmare.

This thought stuck with me overnight. It wasn't going to be a relaxing and chill experience…I was going to be pestered, hounded, and it would not be good. I'd be trapped in awkward encounters… badgered by Billie…my hard-fought serenity, God, maybe even my sobriety, would be at risk. I had no other choice—I'd have to bail on this whole arrangement.

Which I did.

I saw Dave for breakfast at the bakery the next morning and—rather than sign a leasing agreement—explained my apprehension, and, once again, rejected the property. He completely understood. The deal was off.

We shook hands, I left, and went for a long walk in the woods and down to one my favourite beaches, where I sat, staring at Mt. Baker. A few turkey vultures flew overhead, as the waves lapped on the beach. A russet-colored mink scurried over some logs nearby and stopped to look at me, as if to say,

"Don't be an idiot, you'll like it here…what else are you going to do?"

And then I had an epiphany—there are going to be problems, difficulties, wherever you go. There is no escaping them. They are opportunities for growth, and need to be confronted—gently—and dealt with. I can handle this, I told myself. At least try it for a year and if you don't like it you can move on.

I reconnected with Dave and explained my change of heart. Once again, because Dave is a good guy, he completely understood. We met up and I signed the lease for one year…this time, I let the ink dry.

I had found Shavasana.

PostScript:

Billie and I have since become friends and good neighbours. She's big hearted, generous and kind. We look out for one another...and she's right—it's always good to keep a supply of candles handy for those blustery nights when the power can go off.

3

New Year's Eve 1973
—Peshawar, Pakistan

The bus trip from Kabul, Afghanistan to Peshawar, Pakistan is only 300 kilometers and, depending on the mechanical worthiness of your bus, the number of eyes that your bus driver has (ours had only one), the number of herds of goats that cross the road, and the general mood of the border guards (ranging from angry and uncooperative, to indifferent and distracted) the trip should only take between six and 10 hours. And this was in the days before roadside bombs and ambushes.

My travelling companions—four young American men and two young Australian women—and I, arrived in Peshawar mid-afternoon on December 29th…enough time to find a hotel, unload our backpacks, and wander around a bit before grabbing a bite of dinner. We'd been on the road since 7:00 a.m. with limited access to food and only intermittent washroom breaks. There were no washrooms on buses then….and, in fact, often there were no washrooms at all at the various "rest stops". Relieving oneself involved stepping over feces on an open field behind a wall, squatting and pooping.

As it is winter, the countryside here is sparse, arid and brown and we are cold. All of we backpack travelers who are following the Hippie Trail from Istanbul to India are wearing all of our clothing to stay warm. The first Pakistanis we meet seem slightly more affluent than the impoverished Afghanis, and are more fluent in English. Due no doubt to 100 years of British influence during the Raj.

The following day, on December 30, we began exploring our new neighborhood, and according to my Journal, the effects of the world-renowned local hashish, here's an excerpt from my journal:

"...man, these are the craziest days of my life... we are getting so stoned, I bought 1 ounce of hash for about $2.50 from a really paranoid type guy." Unquote.

The astute observations of teenage George. The cultural and sensory differences here, for a young Canadian, are so vast and complete that getting stoned is really unnecessary. Why dilute the intensity of the experience? Why not maintain one's wits in a foreign land where unknown dangers lurk? Chalk it up to hippie culture and blind, youthful invincibility—and of course the fact that I liked to get high. It's what we did…no harm could befall us.

But dangers abound in foreign lands and they take many different forms and seek out unexpected opportunities. The "paranoid guy" that I mentioned related a story about his cousin's "drug bust" in a chai shop for possession of hash. Apparently, he was now stuck in Peshawar continuing to sell drugs to foreigners to help pay for his fine because he had no money. Running afoul of the law in a foreign land is never fun and can be made much worse by corrupt police and officials.

Inappropriate and unwanted advances can also be dangerous—for both parties. When our hash dealer told me that "I had a pretty face" my young straight male desire to defend my sexuality with violence was barely suppressed by my emerging tolerance and worldliness. According to my journal I considered: *"…cutting my hair….but, decided not to because all the guys were getting hit on."*

New Year's Eve 1973. Pakistan and India had been at war three times in 30 years and there was—at that time—a much more noticeable military presence in Pakistan than there was in Afghanistan. Afghanistan was, largely, at peace and would remain so until the Russians invaded in 1979, whereas Peshawar, and Pakistan, felt edgier. It was common to see armed Pashtuns wandering around, and hear random gunshots going off in the near and far. Our hotel was only a short walk from an Arms Bazaar where merchants hawked guns of all kinds and young boys could be seen working away at various weapons manufacturing/assembly jobs.

Our route also took us past open slaughterhouses where children, bathed in blood, would be up to their elbows in entrails, with large knives cutting edible/saleable pieces off lamb and sheep carcasses.

Nothing gets wasted—except for we hippies experiencing this carnage through a hashish-addled fog.

New Year's Eve 1973—Peshawar, Pakistan

We were smoking a lot of hash as we went about our day. Played snooker—smoked hash. Had Lunch—smoked hash. Met a guy selling hashish in Campbell soup cans for us to smuggle back to Canada—decided it was a bad idea, smoked more hash. Eventually our wanderings led us to a carpet shop where we met our new best friend Karwan, the shopkeeper. Our fellow-traveler, Graham, had purchased a $17 carpet, so Karwan showed his appreciation by smoking some hash with us and taking us to his warehouse where he had a section of floor covered in ancient artifacts that he had dug up from a local archaeological site.

"Have a look at these old pieces I have dug up," he said, "if you see something you like, please take it…it is my gift to you."

As backpackers on a long-distance trip, every ounce of weight has significance. I looked around at the various pieces and found a little carved stone head* that I liked, while my buddy Brad picked up an equally attractive small piece that would fit into his pack. We thanked Karwan and he insisted that we join him back in his shop for brandy. It's quite easy to get hash in Pakistan but—as a Muslim country—alcohol is forbidden. But of course, we joined him, thinking it would be rude to do otherwise—adding booze onto our already stoned perspectives.

"Hey Karwan," I asked, "do you know where we can get some booze for tonight? It's New Year's Eve and we're going to have a little party back at our hotel…you could join us…Our other friends will be there too—just bring some of your hash."

Delighted by this invite, Karwan happily gave directions to the store where alcohol could be purchased—in a little bakery just a few blocks away. We told him the name of our hotel and that he could drop in after 8, then we set out in search of the bakery…and alcohol.

It was a nondescript little shop with a few baked goods displayed in the window. We ascended the two stone steps, opened the door and walked in. The owner greeted us warmly, it was late afternoon and most of his wares had been purchased except for some flatbreads and a few sweets. He spoke a little English so we said, "Karwan at the carpet shop said you might have some alcohol for sale?"

Immediately, his cheerful demeanor darkened, the smile left his face and his brows furrowed. His eyes darted from Brad to myself, then he came out from behind the counter, opened the front door and looked up and down the street before shutting the door, pulling down the blinds and locking it.

"One moment please," he said, as he disappeared into the back. He soon reappeared with a bottle of brandy in a bag which he handed to us in exchange for about $5. We thanked him and left…gaining some insight into the paranoia of yesterday's hash dealer…but not enough to make us stop.

We smoked a bit more hash, ate something somewhere and made our way back to our hotel to begin our little New Year's Eve celebration. Graham, Knute, and Brad and I convened in Jill and Sally's room to share the brandy, followed soon after by the arrival of our new friend—Karwan the carpet merchant.

We are doing what young people at parties do in the west…drinking, smoking, sharing laughs, flirting with the girls—vying for their attention while keeping an eye on the competition. It's a small intimate group and we've been travelling together for a month through these foreign lands. Karwan seems to be having fun, drinking and smoking and telling awkward jokes, he could be the foreign student in our college dorm trying to fit in, to be one of the guys and impress the girls.

As midnight approached, we decided to have a New Year's countdown on Graham's watch.

"10-9-8-7-6-5-4-3-2-1… Midnight! Happy New Year!" we all shouted together. Spontaneously, we all gave each other hugs, high fives and handshakes…until I noticed that Karwan wasn't participating in our little celebratory group hug—instead he was sitting on one of the beds looking around rather furtively, with his hands clasped between his legs.

"Go on girls, why don't you give Karwan a hug too?" I suggested.

As Jill reached over to embrace our shopkeeper-friend, he stood up from the bed with a rather obvious erection ballooning out from under his very baggy and loose-fitting white cotton pants. He grabbed Jill, pushed her onto the bed, lay on top of her and began squeezing her breasts vigorously.

Without hesitation, the boys and I grabbed Karwan and peeled him off Jill, and sat him back on the bed so she could escape.

"No, no man, that's not cool," we said to him, "It was just a friendly hug, nothing else intended" "have another drink, it's ok, man."

Someone splashed a bit of brandy in his glass, but between the mistaken expectation of what Karwan thought was happening with two western women in a hotel room, and the embarrassing reality of our collective reaction, he was both humiliated and angry. He lifted his glass to his lips, drank the contents and then smashed it on the floor. At this, we decided that Karwan had overstayed his welcome…we four guys grabbed him by the arms and lift-walked him out the door, down the stairs and outside where we released him…and he fell—unconscious—onto the street in front of our hotel.

We stood there for a while wondering what else to do. Karwan was indeed, passed out on the street. Horses, cars and people slowly made their way around his immobile body. Eventually, the manager of the hotel came out, looked at Karwan, shrugged his shoulders and went back in…according to my journal

"…the hotel guys were supposedly trying to kill him so they let him lie in the street…"

As we grabbed Karwan by the legs and tried to haul him away from the worst of the traffic, a long-haired hippie with a headband and glasses, carrying free beer approached us and said,

"What's all this Brouhaha?"

I turned to the newcomer, accepted one of his beers, and retorted, with comic emphasis, as one does, "Brouhaha!?"

And then—in unison—we all said, "Ha Ha!"

Completing the Firesign Theatre** skit that—as young stoners—we were all familiar with. And then, he was gone. "Maybe I need to cut down on the hash," I thought, as we headed back to the hotel room and our dwindling supply of brandy. I paused briefly, before we entered the Hotel, turned and shouted to the night sky, the only two words in Pashto that I knew, that Brad and I had been taught by two Afghani waiters, in a restaurant in Kabul.

"Chulta Bukharum!" which roughly translates to "kiss my ass". We were young, and we were high and it was New Year's Eve, 1973, in Peshawar, Pakistan.

* *Many years later, back in Vancouver, I took my stone head to the UBC Museum of Archaeology, and was informed that my piece was around 2,000 years old (approximately) and from regional Buddhist archaeological sites*

** *The Firesign Theatre Group, were an American Surreal Comedy Troup popular in the late 60s early 70s, and were known for—amongst other things—the Brouhaha skit*

4

What Fresh Hell is This?

Lesson 1: Let go of attachment and expectation during a Pandemic and an era of Climate Change…

I came to the painful awareness, on or about January 7, 2022, that I had packed on an overabundance of seasonal pounds, developed an undeniable couchlaptop habit, and was feeling—in a word—depranxious.

"Why am I so inert?" I moaned, "Why such difficulty focusing?" I bleated. "Why so little purr in my purpose and so much mean in my meaning?" Faced with this existential angst, I knew what I had to do—call up one of my coffee-shop Shamans for a session. I reached for my iPhone…

Lesson 2: Pause for awareness, take time to assess and understand—go for coffee with a friend

In the Autumn of 2021, I was looking forward to my slower Fall/Winter schedule at my gallery/café on Mayne Island. This was—theoretically—going to free up some time for creative projects that I wanted to work on—a new mask, maybe a painting, definitely some writing, and extra time to refocus on my Podcast, which had been languishing.

Luckily, I did manage to produce a new podcast, and had a fabulous weekend at Shavasana Gallery and Café in mid-November, which coincided with the annual Mayne Island Studio/Art Tour. And then, the Atmospheric River hit.

New terms have shown up recently in our weather lexicon that we have not heard before—Atmospheric River, Heat Dome and Polar Vortex are three relative newcomers that have arrived with their concomitant disasters and associated worries.

The November Atmospheric River Event brought record-breaking amounts of water to BC and Washington State, and catastrophic flooding to the region, which destroyed roads, bridges, dikes, homes, farms, lives and livelihoods. This biblical flooding occurred shortly after Vancouver had a small—but unprecedented—tornado in early November.

We. Don't. Get. Tornados.

And all of this came on the heels of one of our worst summer fire seasons on record when we were introduced to the term "Heat Dome" with its punishing heat and destructive fires. The town of Lytton, several hours drive east of Vancouver was declared "the hottest spot in Canada one day, and then burned to the ground the next".

I had two more sessions with the Gallery on Mayne—early December and mid-December—to pick up some Christmas business and visit with some of my community there. It's a sweet time of year as the walls and shelves of the Gallery are festooned with art and crafts, and the counter is laden with Christmas baking.

Like other regional Cafés, that were not required to ask customers for proof of vaccination, I had adopted a stringent mask policy that allowed people to come in, sit down, take off their masks, and have a coffee. It felt, briefly, like a return to normal. I had even expanded my seating to near full-capacity as coffee shops in Vancouver were doing. It was great—the buzz of happy people visiting and chatting...such a long-awaited relief. But then, in early December, word was reaching us of a new, extremely virulent new variant called "The Omicron" which was coming to spoil the party.

For a while it looked like maybe we were going to be spared—this new variant, which was raging in South Africa and Europe, hadn't hit our shores. But news, and Omicron, travel fast. During my last few days of business in mid-December, conversations started to turn to Xmas party cancellations, and plans to "hunker down" before this next wave of the pandemic—inevitably—hit. By December 14th, we were still hovering around 4300 cases per day (Nationally), and then on the 16th—my last day—they jumped to almost 7,000 cases.

It had arrived. Within ten days we'd be seeing unprecedented numbers like 50 and 55 thousand cases per day. I felt like I was closing up shop and fleeing back to Kitsilano before things got really bad—with half an eye on cancelling my own Christmas plans.

On the ferry back to Vancouver, I had time to reflect on some other tragic news I'd received the day prior. A sweet and gentle man I knew in Kitsilano—a 77-year-old musician named Justis Daniel—

who was operating as the park caretaker at Tatlow Park not far from where I live, had been murdered. There seems to be no shortage of senseless in this world, and this was one more WTF moment to add to my own backpack of worries—an unsolved murder...of a friend...in my neighbourhood.

Despite the stresses of pandemics and regional disasters and senseless murder, life goes on. My partner Cathy and I still had to figure out our Christmas plans. Maybe this is the antidote to tragedy—as the Brits say, "Keep Calm and Carry On"...what else can you do?

"Ok, we'll buy and decorate a tree—that's outdoors so it can't be too risky...right?"..."and gifts?"..."Are they really necessary?" I asked. "Is it worth getting sick, doing all that crowded indoor shopping?"

With lineups and masks and squirt bottles of sanitizers. With furtive, military precision excursions into shops to buy stocking stuffers for your loved ones. Eagerly exiting shops so you can rip off your mask and breathe the cool refreshing air, before planning your next life-threatening purchase....and then, hardest of all, making decisions about Christmas dinner.

A large part of the grueling stress of this pandemic has been the complete overdose of conflicting bits of information and misinformation we've received, the polarization this has created, and the uncertainty this has engendered. As cases of the new Omicron outbreak kept growing exponentially from mid to late December, and with mixed reports coming in on the severity of this particular strain, we were left perplexed about what to do with our six anticipated guests (eight, including ourselves). All info that we were gleaning from our various sources, screamed reduce, diminish, cancel and postpone. The fact that my son and his new wife were flying to Quebec for a four-day excursion, where the outbreak was particularly nasty, and returning Christmas Eve prior to our dinner party—pretty much sealed the decision to not have an indoor sit-down dinner, and instead enact "Plan B". Turkey sandwiches for just we four, meeting in two separate cars in an ocean-side parking lot, to have a little picnic, passing food and visiting through our open windows—despite the snow and minus eight-degree weather! It was...memorable.

It started getting uncharacteristically cold in the third week of December with temperatures below freezing. The Polar Vortex delivered a very rare ten inches of snow on Christmas, followed by a record-breaking -15.3 degrees on the 27th. This bone-chilling cold coincided with our worst-day ever Covid case count, with 49,148 cases nationally, a ten-fold increase in 12 days. Provincial restrictions came back into being, some businesses were shut down, events cancelled, lineups for goods and services returned and—most cruel of all—coffee shops started to limit their indoor seating again, or in my case, close down completely.

    I'm a social animal and, for my mental and emotional well-being, I must get out of the house, and away from my home-office—at least once a day—to interact with the world. Visits with friends at coffee shops plays an important role in that process. By late December, with the Omicron numbers off the charts, indoor seating was not an option and finding someone—anyone—willing to bundle up and sit in subzero weather wasn't happening ...except for my good friend and coffee shop Guru—Jordy B. Our mutual love of coffee and conversation and proximity to each other in Kitsilano has made it relatively easy to scoot out for a cup o' joe and have some of that invaluable human interaction that has been in such short supply—for many—over the past two pandemic years.

    There came a time in early January—a few days—which felt like the emotional low of the past two years. "What exactly is this feeling, this state I'm in?", I wondered, "Is this Ennui?"... "a feeling of listlessness and dissatisfaction arising from a lack of occupation or excitement"...close, but not exactly, maybe it's Lassitude... "a state of physical or mental weariness; lack of energy."...hmm, kinda...Languor?... "the state or feeling, often pleasant, of tiredness or inertia"...no, definitely not, nothing pleasant about this. Torpor?..."a state of physical or mental inactivity; lethargy."...So many terms describing variations of what I'm feeling, but none of them seemed quite bang on. It wasn't Anhedonia..."the inability to feel pleasure."...because I still enjoyed lying on the couch, eating chocolate, and looking at my laptop. There was only one way to find answers to this riddle and break the deadlock of this emotional morass in which I found myself trapped...time to book a session with Jordy B.—my coffee shop Guru.

    "I'll see you at Bucks in 15," came the reply text, "sounds serious, better order a Vente."

    The outdoor seating at Starbucks on West Broadway in Kits has been a cherished meeting place during the pandemic, as it provides a modicum of protection from the elements.

"OK, see ya there," I replied.

"It sounds to me like you're moribund," he said, when I described my plight. "Stagnating...lacking vitality or vigor", "Everybody's been experiencing some version of this...just look at all the shit that's going on...we're two years into a pandemic that's just recently gotten worse...we've had six months of disastrous weather anomalies, almost everybody has overeaten during the festive season...so we're sluggish and justifiably a bit depressed"... "Just recognize it, accept it, forgive yourself and the world for this moment we are all going through...and get your head straight"... "Oh...and, be nice."

Lesson # 3: Forgive Self, Forgive Others and seek forgiveness from others you may have harmed

Always good to sit with JB and receive some of his eclectic wisdom.

"Moribund,"… "yeah, that seems about right," I thought, "and sure, I probably do need to get my head straight."

As I was pondering his last bit of advice to "be nice" and thinking "Hmmm...no, that seems to be asking a bit too much, I don't think I'll do that," a Regional Civil Emergency Advisory Alert came in on our cell phones, blaring out a warning about an impending Tsunami, that had been generated by the Hunga-Tonga-Hunga-Ha'apai volcanic eruption in the south Pacific—the largest volcanic eruption since Krakatoa. We looked up at each other through the steam coming off our hot coffees.

"Well," I said, glancing around, "that galvanizes the ol' Moribundity! Gotta run for higher ground!... See ya!"

All Roads at Any Time

5

Saved by da Mizzles

It was late summer, 1973, and I was a long-haired 18-year-old kid about to embark on my post high school round-the-world odyssey of personal discovery…and fun. In preparation for the cross-Canada train trip from Vancouver to Montreal—where my best friend Keith and I would catch our flight to Amsterdam—I decided to leave my parent's home in Victoria and stay in Vancouver for a few weeks, where my brother-in-law had arranged short-term, shared accommodation for me at his secretary's apartment.

Barb was a much older single mother of one (she was 23), and carries the distinction of being the woman to whom I lost my virginity in the days and weeks prior to my departure for distant lands.

"Wow, this is great!" I thought, "exotic travel <u>and</u> sex…I should've left Mom and Dad's place years ago"

What the parental home may lack in terms of exotic and erotic freedom is oftentimes compensated for by its protective cocoon—my first sexual encounter would also be my first (but sadly not my last) encounter with venereal disease. Young—but not yet worldly—Georgie had "the clap".

Aah, but I was not bitter or angry (after all, I'd finally had sex), and the clinic loaded me up with enough pharmaceuticals to kill a horse and also ensure that I would catch my train on time. Thank God for antibiotics…and sex!

If you've ever caught the train across Canada you'll know—but it bears repeating—that it's an absolutely gorgeous journey and a very leisurely and civilized way to travel. Grand Canadian vistas viewed from spacious seating areas through large picture windows.

Because Keith and I were budget travelers we did not rent a stateroom choosing instead to spend the four-day trip either wandering to the dining car or residing in our ample seats…this, of course, left us exposed to interactions with the other passengers. Late one evening, before we pulled into Montreal, a fellow, whom we'd never seen before, approached us with an offer of free drugs—some kind of hallucinogenic, in powdered format. Being young hippie-ish kids with a fondness for getting high, and an—evidently—undeveloped sense of self-preservation, readily agreed and ate, a spoonful or two, each, of the foreign substance. We ingested as much as his largesse would allow, and, after hanging out with us for a short while, he got up and left for another passenger compartment, never to be seen again.

We waited…patiently. After a time, I said:

"I'm not feeling anything…you?"

"No," replied Keith, "I wonder what that shit was?"

We remained in our seats with our advancing disappointment, and mild apprehension.

"Maybe it was baking soda," said Keith.

"Or poison…rat poison," I countered.

Either way, apprehension is not an ideal state from which to enjoy a good night's sleep. We arrived in Montreal feeling a little burnt out but eager to embark on the next stage of our journey—transatlantic flight! Europe! Yay!

By the time we got to the airport, checked our backpacks, boarded the plane and lifted off from the tarmac, I started to notice that I wasn't feeling so great. I had a mild headache, felt slightly feverish and had increasing difficulty swallowing. My throat felt constricted and scratchy.

"I might be coming down with a cold," I told my buddy Keith.

"That's a drag man, why don't you ask the stewardess if they have any pills for that?"

"Great idea," I thought, "that's all I need is some kind of medicine." A pill for every ill. "Uhhh, stewardess!"

The ever obliging and helpful stewardess (in the days before flight attendants) hauled out her bag of pharmaceuticals and gave me two of something to ease my plight. Painstakingly I swallowed them, not thinking for a moment that perhaps, just perhaps, adding more chemicals into my system on top of the recent antibiotics and "mystery drug" might be unwise. I thanked her and smiled flirtatiously in my new role as a non-virgin.

Not surprisingly, the pills didn't work and, by the time we landed in Amsterdam, on a Sunday, I was feeling considerably worse and now had a noticeable rash on my torso comprising of small raised red spots.

"Hey man, I don't know what I've got," I said, "but I feel like shit and think I need to have this looked at…let's ditch our backpacks at the Hostel and go find a doctor."

"Where are we going to find a doctor on a Sunday…in a foreign country?" replied Keith.

Remember, it's 1973…no internet…no smartphones or handy apps…we didn't even have credit cards. American Express cheques, a copy of the Lonely Planet Guide, and the optimism of youth were the tools with which all obstacles would be overcome.

"We'll ask the guy at the Hostel, c'mon."

"Red Light District, …you can find anything you want in the Red Light District," said the Hostel Guy. "Here" …he slid a piece of paper across the reception desk, with an address on it, making sure not to touch my hand for fear of infection.

God bless the Dutch…and their multilingualism (Hostel Guy spoke impeccable English), and their progressive ways! "Anything we want"…on a Sunday no less, how civilized. We made our way into Amsterdam's world-famous "Rosse Buurt" seeking medical salvation.

The unabashed display of prostitution and open accessibility of soft drugs made me forget—momentarily—that I was dying of an unnamed illness. For two parochial lads from the repressive Social Credit province of British Columbia, seeing bars open—and serving alcohol—on a Sunday was perhaps even more of a revelation to the permissive wonderland of vice that the Dutch had created. I knew I was going to like it here—if I survived my plague.

Armed with a roughly drawn map, showing us the short walkable distance between the Hostel and the Rosse Buurt, we headed out. Marijuana smoke wafted out from Sleezy Bars, scantily clad hookers sat behind picture windows plying their trade, garish neon signs announced "Live Sex Shows—Real Fucky Fucky", next door to leather bondage gear and sex toy shops.

"I think we've strayed from the recommended sites of the Official Tourist Guide," I said, "are we almost there?"

"I think so," said Keith, "according to Hostel Guys instructions it's just a bit further up Nieuwezijds Voorburgwal …c'mon"

The doctor's office was on the second floor of a three-storey brick and stone walk up. Down a poorly lit hallway, the wooden door with the frosted pane read: Dr. Willem de Ridder, Room 216. I knocked. A gravelly male voice said, "Kom Binnen". Inside the room, sitting behind a wooden office desk with a cigarette in his mouth, sat the Doctor, languidly petting the head of a Red Setter. The room was stale with cigarette smoke and on the desk sat an ashtray full of cigarette butts. Between cigarettes and strokes of his faithful pet's head, the doctor explored my throat and infected torso with his nicotine-stained fingers. "I sink you haff an infection", he said, "I vill give you some pills—antibiotica—which vill clear up your problem in a few days". Being the trusting sort: of older, more experienced women; of strangers on a train; of the medical acumen of stewardesses; and of doctors in Red Light Districts...on a Sunday—I took the pills.

Back on the street, we decided to go back to the Hostel for a while and chill out as we were both suffering from a bit of jet lag and overall travel fatigue. Combined with my indeterminate illness, I felt a need to lie down and let my new pharmaceuticals work their magic.

The bar looked seedy and non-descript. An open doorway into darkness with early 70s era rock pounding from within. As we attempted to pass, a half dozen young Moluccan* males—some with knives hanging from their belts—exited the bar and surrounded us in a circle.

"Eyyy man, where you boys be goin?" said the ringleader, "You got no need to be runnin' off...why don' choo c'mon into da bar an buy us a drink man?"

Parochial or otherwise, Keith and I both knew what it meant to be surrounded by a slightly intimidating pack of males. This kind of threat plays out in schoolyards around the world and is not an uncommon experience for young males everywhere—the knives were an unfamiliar twist.

"My friend is sick and needs to lie down—we're going to the Hostel," said Keith, going for the sympathy play. Unconvinced, our "new best drinking buddies" shuffled a bit and looked slyly at each other, without any sign of backing down. Realizing that they needed further convincing, and in one momentarily clever strategic move, I lifted my t-shirt up to my chest to expose my torso, which was covered in bright red spots.

"Whoa man, you gots da mizzles!" said the ringleader, now with a tone of fear and dread.

He and his cronies had all immediately taken about five steps backwards when they saw me covered with an apparent communicable illness.

"You gonna need a doctor…go dat way" he pointed further down the street, as he and his mates slunk back into the bar—defeated by "da mizzles".

Feeling relieved by this narrow escape, we carried on with "Plan A" and made our way back to the sanctuary of the Youth Hostel.

"How're you feeling man?", asked Keith, "Shitty," I replied,

Later that night, I lay in my dormitory style metal bunk bed, fully clothed, wrapped in my sleeping bag, shivering, shaking, and bathed in sweat from fever and mild delirium. The red spots had now spread to my groin, upper arms and back. The first day of my overseas adventure had taken some unexpected twists.

It would be a few years before I made the connection between my pharmaceutical overdose—too many chemicals in too short a time—and my "mystery illness", longer still before I understood the political plight of young Moluccan* men in the Netherlands.

Despite my near-death pharmaceutical misadventure, we got lucky on this day and may have accidentally been saved by 'da mizzles'…more reliable street smarts would definitely be required to get us safely through the rest of this trip.

* *(The Moluccans are a people from the Maluku Islands, an archipelago in Eastern Indonesia. When Indonesia gained independence from the Dutch in 1950, The Republic of Maluku tried to secede, supported by the Netherlands. When the movement was defeated, 12,000 Moluccans were transported to Holland where "They were then discharged on arrival, not allowed to work, given pocket money and 'temporarily' housed in camps." Because "the Dutch government, never made any effort to help the Moluccans establish their Republik," this marginalization "radicalised young Moluccans in the Netherlands, during the '70s, which included a train hijacking in 1975, taking hostages at De Punt in Groningen, and at a school in Bovensmilde."*

All Roads at Any Time

6

"Why Don't You Just Kill Rambo?"

Rambo Barked at Butterflies
Rambo Barked at Bees
Rambo Barked at Sunshine and the cool Autumn breeze
He lunged and snapped at babies
Fangs bared at you and me
Rambo Barked at everything
Die now Rambo…die now… please?

We suspect that the Real Estate agent asked the neighbours to hide their dog Rambo in their house while she was showing her listing to prospective purchasers, such as I and my 8 and a half months pregnant wife Elaine, on that sunny but crisp February morning.

We were a young couple with a baby on the way and this was our first house purchase so we were operating at maximum busy, excited and optimistic. Perhaps—because of this—we weren't as attentive to important details, such as the character and compatibility of our new neighbours, but on that day, none of that mattered, all seemed well, and our offer was made…and accepted. We were the new owners of a sweet little stucco bungalow on West 17th Avenue in Vancouver!

We took possession quickly, loaded up a truck with our belongings, and enlisted the help of friends to make setting up our nest as smooth and fun as possible.

I don't remember when Rambo started barking. We were so busy in those early days, setting up house, working at our respective jobs, buying baby things, and getting ready for Elaine's due date—which was just weeks away—that everything else dropped off the radar. We'd met our new neighbours—a seemingly pleasant, middle-age

Greek couple—who ran a restaurant up on Broadway, and were the proud parents of five daughters ranging in age from six to 16. And we were vaguely aware that they owned a rather large German Shepherd which seemed confined to their back yard.

Dogs bark, it's normal for them to do so, and is part of the background noise/fabric of city life...lots of people...lots of dogs...lots of barking. I like dogs—a lot—and always try and befriend them wherever I go. In fact, I'm a complete idiot when it comes to dogs and will crouch down on one knee in the street if I see someone walking a dog in hopes that I can pet them..."Do you mind if I say hello to your dog?", I implore, "Oh yes, go right ahead, Bart (or Fluffy or Rex) is very friendly"...and then it's all sweet luvvins, hugs, and ear rubs. Rarely am I warned off with, "No no, please maintain your distance...Satan is trained to kill and will lunge for your throat without a moment's warning."—but there are such dogs.

Our son was born on March 11, just weeks after we had moved into our new home. The delivery went smoothly and soon we were cuddling and fawning over 8 pounds 13 ounces of joy that would transform our lives. Elaine only needed a day or so in the hospital before she and our new baby Cameron were deemed safe to come home.

A typical Vancouver lot is 33' feet wide by 120' long. Usually, there is a narrow three or four-foot strip along one side of the house, with a sidewalk—allowing for access to the back yard—and a fence separating the neighbouring property. We parked on the street and for some reason decided to walk along this sidewalk with Cam bundled up in my arms, to enter via the back door. It was a lovely day, and Elaine walked on ahead as I navigated the narrow sidewalk while learning how to safely carry a baby.

Suddenly and unexpectedly, 80 pounds of German Shepherd ferocity was standing full-height on its back legs, with its front paws leaning over the fence, lunging, snapping and barking—fangs bared—within inches of our days-old baby's head. I automatically turned to face the stucco wall, pressing Cam closer to my body as I crab walked sideways into the back yard, with our faces almost scraping the stucco, in an effort to avoid Rambo's bite.

Elaine turned in horror as I scrambled to safety with Cam.

"God, are you guys OK?" She asked, as I handed Cameron to her. Who was, by the way, still sleeping and completely nonplussed by the situation.

"That scared the shit outta me," I said. "We're going to have to have a chat with the neighbours" "Be super careful if you ever need to walk alongside the house until we get this sorted out."

That evening, I wandered over and rang Dmitri's doorbell. One of his daughters answered the door and called out, "Dad!" We had already met the neighbours and they seemed like very amicable people. When Dmitri appeared, I explained our scary and dangerous encounter with his threatening dog and he was most apologetic.

"Oh no…we are so sorry about that…and with the new baby," he said, "Rambo is very protective of my girls and we have him because we work late at our restaurant. He keeps our girls safe when they are home alone. He's just not used to you yet as you are new." "We'll keep him on the back deck so he won't lean over the fence at you again…so sorry,"

Thus assured, I went home and told Elaine about the "solution to our little problem". All seemed well.

The next few months were a haze of new parenthood, settling into our new digs and grappling with all the demands that life throws at 30-somethings in the late 1980s. We discovered—quite quickly—that "Rambo's deck" was on the back of the neighbour's house, on the same side and level as our bedroom…about 10 to 15 feet away from where we would be—trying—to sleep…and that, as well as his violent demeanor, Rambo was an incessant barker.

I have a gift. It is the gift of sleep, and I am blessed to be able to sleep almost anywhere and through nearly all conditions. Noise had never been an impediment to sleep—until Rambo. And I should explain that in fact it wasn't Rambo's barking that woke me up at night but Elaine's sharp elbow and insistent voice.

"George" jab jab "George!" jab jab "GEORGE!" "Rambo's barking and it's going to wake the baby" "That's every night this week."

"Uuh…ok," I said rousing from my deep sleep…"what do you suggest?"

"That dog has been barking almost constantly since we moved in two months ago…it can't go on… between breastfeeding Cameron and Rambo's barking I'm not getting any sleep" "Why don't you go over and knock on their door and ask them to keep their dog quiet?"

"It's only 2:00 a.m., I don't think Dmitri or Sophia are back from the restaurant," I replied, hoping it would spare me from doing the requested task.

"Well then, go and talk to one of the daughters, they can deal with it."

"Uuh... ok, ok" I said pulling myself out of bed. I slipped on my housecoat and some shoes and headed out.

Most of the houses on the street were built in the 1940's and 50s and were equipped with the "old school" round white plastic doorbell button. I pushed it twice. Then a third time before I could hear the sounds of someone stirring inside, against the background of Rambo's—now feverish—barking. A young girl's trembling voice came through the door

"Who is it?" she asked.

"Hi," I said, "It's George your next-door neighbour...Hey, Rambo is barking a lot and it's waking our baby...Can you bring him inside or something?"

"Oh, sorry," she said. I think it was the 12-year-old. "Ok, I'll bring him in."

"Thank you! G'night," I replied.

Problem solved, I thought. It seemed like such a simple solution—just bring Rambo into the house at night as we were all getting ready to go to sleep...ahh...I felt a wave of relief, and satisfaction that I had effectively completed my "man duty" and protected my family from this noisy disruptive beast. Going one step further, I vowed to get their phone number in case I was ever in such a situation again and would just phone, rather than looking like a sketchy guy in a housecoat standing on a porch at 2 in the morning.

The "system" seemed to work—for a while. Rambo was still a crazy threatening barkaholic from his porch, but the girls made an effort to bring him in at night, and if they forgot, I could just phone and they would oblige. But then, they seemed to lose the thread of the agreement and either forgot to bring him in at night or just wouldn't answer the phone.

After several more months of this hit and miss solution, as Elaine's late night elbow jabs were becoming more frequent and insistent and I was becoming more irritated at the neighbour's intransigence, I came up with the bright idea that perhaps I could recondition Rambo not to bark through negative reinforcement—or punishment—in layman's terms.

We left the hose out at all times and I would turn the tap on and spray Rambo anytime we felt he was going into 'overbark'. Cunning beast that he was, he figured this game out fairly quickly and would go to the other end of the porch to avoid the cold water and continue barking. Late one night, I got out of bed to have a cigarette and spray Rambo when Dmitri—who happened to be home—leaned out the window and said,

"Hey! Why are you spraying my dog?"

"Well Dmitri", I said, taking a slow pull from my cigarette, "He sounds like he's getting a little hoarse from all the constant barking!"

"No one answered the phone when I called."

"We didn't hear the phone," he replied.

"Well, can you take him in now?" I asked.

"No, he's all wet."

I put the hose down and went inside, angry. 'The system,' which also included civility, seemed to be breaking down.

Elaine had gone back to work after her maternity leave ended but we were still wrestling with "the Rambo problem" after a year of seeking possible solutions. We griped about this situation to friends, family, and coworkers because it had become a seemingly insoluble problem that we were obsessed with. During one dinner party after a few glasses of wine our friend Dave said,

"Why don't you just kill Rambo?"

We all paused at this suggestion, and looked at Dave to see if he was serious.

"Sure, you just need some kind of poison, wrap it in a piece of steak and chuck it up on the porch," he continued.

After this length of time, it almost seemed like a good idea, but no, we couldn't do that—we both liked dogs too much to even contemplate such an act, and realized that this wasn't really Rambo's fault, it was the owner's fault, because they hadn't trained him properly and weren't dealing with a viable solution.

"Maybe we could kill Dmitri and Sophia," I suggested, eliciting a raucous laugh from our guests who were used to my dark sense of humor.

"I may have a solution for you guys," said Elaine's co-worker Milo.

Milo was a very clever guy who was a skilled technician with BC Tel.

"I could set up a high pitch sound feedback device, that would blast Rambo with a high pitch noise, only audible to a dog's ears, every time he barked" "It's kind of an immediate feedback loop…his bark triggers a switch on a noise sensor which triggers the other high pitch noise amplifier" "Essentially the high pitch noise would hurt his hearing and train him not to bark through negative feedback."

"Wow," said Elaine and I in unison, "What a cool idea Milo, I mean, it sounds like a long shot but we're willing to try anything."

Within days the affable and earnest Milo returned with the device which he had fabricated in his workshop at home. He had even attached it to a wall bracket which would screw into the side of our house, close to our bedroom window so we could run a power chord to an inside wall plug. It looked a little cumbersome, like a 1950s Sci-Fi illustration of a death ray machine, and if that was the net result, we would not be heartbroken, but we were hoping that Milo's hi-tech solution proved worthy of its promise…we plugged it in.

Rambo, of course, had been barking incessantly since Milo showed up, enraged by the appearance of this stranger doing strange things in our yard. When the device was finally installed and plugged in, we all held our breath, hoping that Rambo would collapse in a puddle of furry whimpering discomfort with each bark.

We watched closely, trying to detect any sign of "negative feedback loop effect" which might indicate that Milo's device was working.

"I think I saw him wince," I said.

"He's got a kind of puzzled quizzical look…I think," said Elaine.

"Maybe I need to turn it up to 11," said Milo.

"Yes! Yes!" we agreed, "11-12-19—max it out Milo! Let's see what this baby can do."

After a few more tweaks and adjustments, we all stood in the yard, intently looking at Rambo, which infuriated him into a spasm of frothy barking.

Whatever behavioural modification benefits the inflicted pain might have given us seemed to be offset by the additional frenzy Rambo was exhibiting from receiving it. This new discomfort just made him crazier, plus, wily beast that he was, he moved farther back on the deck, seemingly to get away from the "range of pain".

"Give it a week," said Milo, "It'll take a little while to see if it works."

We gave it a month, it didn't work, and we fell into some kind of despair.

"Well honey, we've tried everything," said Elaine, "Do you think it's time to exercise the "Dave Option?"

"No, I can't even seriously contemplate that," I said, "There is the Noise By-Law Infraction." "Maybe it's time to get City Hall on our side, show Dmitri and Sophia we mean business. Hit 'em in the pocketbook where it hurts, with a big fat fine. Leave this one to me, honey, I'll call the City."

The Vancouver City Dog Barking Noise By-Law Infraction process is, in itself, a descent into a Kafkaesque bureaucratic nightmare. After 18 months of frustration and fruitless effort, this appeared to be the last avenue open to us—short of exercising the "Dave Option". A labyrinth of paperwork, identifications, reporting, discussions and explanations, delays and perhaps most unfair of all, the need to "Use a log (called a barking package) to record the day, time, and duration of barking, and impact it has on you" which was, at that time, several months of required record-keeping. If the Animal Control Officer thinks you have a case, it goes to the City Prosecutor to set up a Court Date, which you must attend and if successful a Fine is set. From start to finish this whole process took about four or five months, countless hours of my time, and in the end, they were fined $75 for a first offence—with a warning.

And all the while, Rambo barked and barked and barked.

"Well, that was a complete waste of time," I said, with resignation, "Five months of effort and they get a $75 fine and a warning, and our problem hasn't gone away" "How shitty is that?"

We sat in the front room and looked out the picture window as two-year-old Cam played happily with his toys, as toddlers do.

"Maybe they'll make more of an effort to control Rambo," said Elaine, "If we continue with the noise bylaw, the fines get heavier and I think they can have their dog impounded."

"Money doesn't seem to be a problem for those guys," I said, "And if Rambo gets impounded, they'd probably just get a bigger, meaner, noisier dog to protect the girls from monsters at night…a Rottweiler with a personality disorder…or a Mastiff with Childhood Trauma…something so psychotic and big we'd never be able to sleep or access our sidewalk again."

Elaine could tell I was embellishing for playful effect…and she smiled.

"I dunno," she said, "I guess for the time being we have to go back to square one and call them at night if we're woken up…what other option do we have, being as you're too cowardly to do the manly thing and go over there and break Rambo's neck?"

Now it was my turn to smile. "Yeah, let's just take it one day at a time," I said, "I guess we'll need a fresh supply of earplugs."

Whatever reprieve we were hoping for was short-lived: 2:00 a.m., days after the Court decision. Bark Bark Bark! Jab-Jab-Jab…

"George, Rambo's barking!"

"I know, I know, you don't have to jab me with your elbow anymore, I hear him, you've effectively conditioned me to be as noise sensitive as you," I said testily, "I always hear him…there is no escape," I said with bitter resignation.

And from down the hall…Waaah Waaah Waahh!

"And Cameron's crying, he's probably still a bit feverish," I said, "Why don't you go deal with Camy, and I'll try calling the neighbours."

I threw on my housecoat and went to the phone where the Kakavelakis families' number was written on a yellow sticky note.

Bark! Bark! BARK! went Rambo…Waaa Waaah! WAAAH! Went Cameron. Bark! BARK! Waah! WAAH! …BARK! WAH! BARK! WAH!

I thought I was losing my mind as I anxiously dialed their number.

Ring Ring Ring! Ring Ring Ring! Ring BARK WAH Ring! Please God make it stop!

Then, someone picked up the phone. There was no greeting so I just launched in.

"Hi, it's George next door," I said, "our little boy is not feeling well and Rambo's barking is disturbing his sleep…and ours". There was no reply, a brief hesitation, and then they hung up the phone.

Where does mercurial anger start? From the toes? Does it build and flow from our extremities? Rushing carelessly like a raging river through our veins, gaining strength as it cascades through our hearts on its way to the brain where it explodes and washes away the dykes and dams of learned civil behaviour?

The pent-up anger and frustration of two years of dealing with this issue boiled over and I "totally lost my shit" as they say. I grabbed my shoes and headed out the door.

"J'en ai Ras le Bol Tabarnak!" I swore in my passable Quebeois. "Hang up on me when I've got a sick baby, you fuckers!" I muttered under my breath. Having a sick baby can add a sense of righteousness to indignant rage, so I definitely pulled that card out of my anger deck.

I marched across their lawn and ran up their stairs and began leaning on the doorbell.

"Ding-Dong Ding-Dong DING-DONG!"

I didn't let up on this for several minutes, and it's probably good that no one came to the door—I had become the monster that Dmitri was trying to protect his family from—an enraged man who had taken leave of his senses. While on the porch I started kicking their aluminum screen door as well, putting a sizeable dent into the lower half, and then, realizing it might be time to leave before the police showed up, casually kicked all their potted plants off their front steps on my way back down.

Good thing I wasn't drunk or it could've gotten…ugly.

The next morning, we sat in the kitchen having coffee, discussing this new escalation in events. I think Elaine may have been secretly pleased by my outburst, because it served as a long overdue release of her own pent-up frustration and anger, but also horrified because it represented a new low in our neighbourly relations.

"I totally get why you did that," she said, "we've really been put through the wringer on this, if I hadn't been looking after Camy, I might've gone over and gotten into some kind of scrap with those guys myself." "Now, it's not just Rambo we have to worry about…it's Dmitri's reaction, and our emotional well-being"

"God, what if he gets a second dog for the front yard to protect his girls from late-night angry neighbours?" I pondered, "Sigh, such a shitty situation…I don't even like living here anymore…any ideas?"

We sat for a while in silence, sipping our coffees and pondering our situation when there was a knock at the door.

"Shit, that's probably Dmitri coming to chew me out and seek restitution for damages, I'll get it," I said.

I opened the door and there was a smiling bright faced woman with short blond hair, holding some pamphlets.

"Hi," she said, "My name's Sue Clayton-Carroll, I'm a local realtor, and I'm dropping off some flyers because I just sold a house down the street, which is quite like yours, for $250,000, and I'm checking to see if you have any interest in selling."

My eyes widened at this amount—maybe I salivated a bit—as it was fully double what we'd paid just two short years ago. I could see, out of the corner of my eye, Elaine sit bolt upright on the couch when she heard the amount.

"Hi Sue," she said, "I'm Elaine, I co-own this house with George…so…if we wanted to sell with you, would you be willing to ask our next door neighbour to take their dog Rambo indoors during the Open House? He's a little noisy."

"Oh, I'm sure that wouldn't be a problem," said Sue, "We realtors are asked to do that all the time."

7

The Blüthner

It was just sitting there, waiting for me, when I got back from Vancouver. Black, lustrous, and beautiful, it now occupied the space I'd left for it against the far wall between the two tall blond cabinets. Possessing a certain presence and grace, it sat there patiently, as if expecting me. My new roommate had arrived—the Blüthner piano was here.

The movers had obviously found the "secret key" and managed to access my Gallery and wrestle its awkward bulk into place, without my assistance. For this I was grateful, as pianos are notoriously difficult to move. Three-men with a truck, a special dolly and straps are still no guarantee of safety—for the piano or the movers. This is why you'll find many pianos being offered for "free"—if you pick up the moving fees.

In fact, the piano was not mine—a friend had received it, for free, when the local Community Centre on Mayne Island decided to divest themselves of their two pianos. His impulsive agreement to take the piano was short-lived though, when he realized that he didn't have space for it. Pianos are beautiful instruments and have an intrinsic allure, even if you don't know how to play them—like myself. When offered a chance to "store it indefinitely" in my Gallery Café, I readily accepted, and now, it was here…what to do?

It looked lovely in its new home, fitting perfectly between the two cabinets, allowing for stylish art displays on the wall in the alcove above, and on top of the piano too. But what of the piano itself? What is a Blüthner? A name I'd never heard—before one showed up in my Gallery. I was curious.

It all starts with a little Wikipedia…

"*Julius   Blüthner   Pianofortefabrik* *manufactures   pianos* in Leipzig Germany. Along with Bechstein, Bösendorfer, and Steinway, Blüthner is frequently referred to as one of the "Big Four" piano manufacturers. Established in 1853, Julius Blüthner, a deeply religious man, spoke the defining words that would allow his company to survive and flourish for the next 169 years, "May God Prevail". The age of any particular Blüthner piano can be determined by matching its serial number to the age table freely available on the Blüthner website."

Blüthner pianos have won international awards consistently since their inception, and have been prized by pianists all over the world, including Rachmaninoff who said, "There are only two things which I took with me on my way to America...my wife and my precious Blüthner".

"Hmm...that's an impressive pedigree," I thought "...and I can determine the age of my Blüthner?.. That's so cool..."

I had to look. Lifting up the lid, and exposing the Hammer Action I saw the Serial number stencilled on the metal frame, "92989" Returning to the computer and the Blüthner website I was able to determine that my Blüthner was built in 1914—exactly 100 years earlier (I was doing all this sleuthing in March, 2014).

100 years. I paused to reflect for a moment on this significant date. I think we naturally accredit a special respect for anything that is celebrating a century of life on this earth. If the Blüthner was not technically alive, it had experienced a lot of life at the hands of its various owners. And, significantly, it was born in Leipzig Germany at the start of World War 1 which began on July 28th of that year.

A few questions immediately sprung to mind: "Where did it go?" "What circuitous route—throughout its 100 years—brought it to Mayne Island?"

My curiosity about the Blüthner's journey was piqued and I wanted to know all I could about her...but all I had was the piano sitting before me—and she wasn't speaking. I grabbed a flashlight and a screwdriver and started to explore.

Removing the bottom panel just above the piano pedals I peered in with my flashlight and saw the Serial number again, handwritten in pencil along with what appeared to be a signature. My first thought was of a young German piano maker leaving his mark for posterity—a little Saxon graffiti—and immediately wondered what might have happened to him with the advent of War.

Without knowing for certain though, I sent a photo to my German friend Rainer Schroeder of Valhalla Tours, for translation. Rainer said that although "it's definitely a word...the font is in Old German "Suetterlin" and he wasn't sure what it meant".

Undaunted, I went online and found Katherine Shober of S.K. Translations who works in this field to see if she could help – Katherine was too busy but directed me to Geneologist Dr. Ellen Yutzy Glebe. She too was busy but gave me three Facebook Translation Groups—which I joined—and within hours had a viable translation from Georg Patrzek—"It looks like "Tschempel" which is an old German family name" he said, ...God I love the internet.I was glad that the word I'd discovered was a family name and didn't mean "right piano leg" in **Sütterlinschrif** . Knowing that Mr. or Mrs. Tschempel decided to sign this instrument upon which he (or she) worked creates a whole thread of historic inquiry to ponder or pursue. Was he young, old, married with family? What happened to Tschempel? Did he get sent to fight in World War I? Or World War II?—in a last grasp at trying to understand, and complete this circle, I sent an inquiry to the Blüthner Piano Company, which still operates in Leipzig to this day. Within fairly short order, I received a polite reply from someone in their Public Relations department that they did not keep employee records dating back that far, but they did thank me for my inquiry.Realizing that I'd hit a bit of a dead end with regards to the identity or history of Mr. Tschempel, I turned my attention back to the piano. The next and most obvious clue in the Blüthner's journey was a small metal plaque attached to the keyboard lid which read, "Bowran and Co. Ltd—Newcastle on Tyne"

I knew that Newcastle on Tyne was in England, so the Blüthner had to have made its way safely between two warring countries, but I had no way of knowing when it made that perilous trip. Mr. Google was there to help and gave me a little tidbit from the Newcastle Journal August 4th, 1916...a small classified ad indicating that E.O. Bowran was indeed engaged in piano sales, representing several makes and models of new and used pianos. Bowran survived the war but not the great Depression, and had to be "wound up due to liabilities", as published in the London Gazette, February 5, 1935

So, somewhere between 1914 and 1935, the Blüthner made its way to England, sat in a Piano Shop in Newcastle upon Tyne and was sold either new, used or as part of a bankruptcy liquidation.

Sometime during its long life, an aspiring pianist, or perhaps a child who didn't know better, sat down at the piano with a pen and piece of paper, and forever scarred the keyboard cover while writing out the notes and lyrics to a song. All I have been able to discern from this etching on the piano are these words and chords:

"Bridge...Bb...Crazy...on...After...Em...Let's...on...Bill...Dean ...Eb... F#m ...D"

Their scribbling moved around too much for me to identify the song, or tell what era it's from. I visualize a young student or budding musician from the 60's or 70's copying or creating a piece for personal enjoyment or to entertain family and friends. I find these words add a human element to the Blüthner's almost indecipherable journey.

The trail goes cold here until August 10, 1986, when, according to a sticker I found attached to the inside of the piano, the Blüthner was tuned up by a man named Cliff Brownlee of Penticton, British Columbia.

I've attempted to fill in some of the gaps in the Blüthner's history but haven't been able to go beyond the plaques, stickers, and graffiti that were left attached to the piano. The 50-year gap between Newcastle and Penticton is long so I decided to try and locate Cliff Brownlee in Penticton to see if he was still alive and if he could remember anything about the piano—a full 28 years after his tuning job. It was—a long shot.

Much to my surprise, I found him in the Penticton directory, no longer listed as a piano tuner and living at a different address but still alive and accessible. I felt compelled to call him. What possible harm could it do, I thought? Again, surprisingly, Cliff picked up the phone after a couple of rings. I could tell by his voice that I was not dealing with a young man. I explained who I was and why I was calling—that I was on a crazy mission to try and understand the life of a piano. How did it get to Penticton?...and then to Mayne Island?

Cliff was friendly but admitted that—after this length of time—he really had very little memory of working on the Blüthner, but—again with the surprises—he said he would look into his files, and call me back. He did just that. Two days later I received a call from him, unfortunately, he wasn't able to elaborate much more on my pianos journey. He did recall coming to Mayne to tune a Grand Piano back when he was still in business, so we speculated that perhaps the Blüthner was here at that time, and not in Penticton, and that Cliff had picked up some additional tuning jobs.

I had one more lead to try—call the Community Centre and see where they got the piano and talk to whomever donated it. A chat with Lauren led to me Lise who gave me the final word on my quest. A couple named Don and Nina T. had made the donation to the Community Centre but they were now both in a seniors care facility in Victoria and should really not be disturbed. The thought being that perhaps they would be dismayed to know that their "donation" had changed hands and was now in a Gallery Café.

After all my sleuthing I certainly had the urge to call them, or their family members, but I honoured Lise's request to leave them in peace. If Don and Nina's intent when they made their donation was for the Blüthner to be cared for and played lovingly, I'm sure they would love the little video that I made called, "Eleven Pieces for the Blüthner".** It's a compilation, made over five or six years of people dropping by the café and asking if it would be OK to sit down and play a few pieces for the customers. I'm sure the enthusiasm and talent of the performers and the evident appreciation of their various audiences would warm Don and Nina's hearts, and assuage any concerns they may have…

** *If you are at all interested in viewing/listening to this 5-minute compilation, it can be viewed on my Shavasana Art Gallery and Café website: shavasana.ca got to Blogs February 6, 2020.*

All Roads at Any Time

8

Transient Epileptic Amnesia

It's difficult to say with any certainty, exactly when I developed Transient Epileptic Amnesia (TEA). My feeling is that it began with my decision to quit drinking—cold turkey—after a particularly excessive and toxic stag-party in Vegas in 2010. Three days later, back in Vancouver, I was getting out of bed and suffered my first seizure, which resulted in my collapsing in the hallway and breaking my right ankle. This was labelled an Alcohol Withdrawal Syndrome seizure by the Emergency Room doctor as he was tending to my—first—broken foot. "Who knew?"... that you shouldn't quit drinking suddenly, and that it was better to wean oneself gradually off the booze. In fact, I was trying to detoxify so I could drive to Burning Man Festival the following week.

The Emergency Room Doctor's explanation made complete sense, it was viewed as a one-off, and I vowed to never quit drinking again.

All kidding aside, I was almost grateful that this event had arrived. One would think that—seizure, collapse, broken foot, crutches and a boot—would be a significant enough message for me, to finally quit drinking—forever. "Thank God," I thought, "here's the wake-up call that I need to genuinely tackle my drinking problem, once and for all."

I lasted six months before I was back at it hammer and tongs.

Fast forward to May 2012, a full month after I had joined the AA program and finally gained my sobriety. I awoke disoriented one day but attached no particular significance to this. I was experiencing a brief difficulty with short-term memory and was peppering my partner with questions about what had transpired the week prior and what was coming up. Other than a little generalized confusion, my thought was that this was just my brain adjusting to life without alcohol. I wasn't hung-over and this was unusual. After a half an hour of this I shrugged it off as an inconsequential result of quitting drinking. All good—I thought.

A month later it happened again. The symptoms were similar but this time it lasted a bit longer—long enough for me to get dressed, leave the house and go grab a coffee. The world appeared slightly changed and both the visuals and the smells were different. I felt like I was a little high. It was slightly hallucinatory but this too dissipated with time, and I chalked it up to further evidence of my post-alcoholic healing. Although I wasn't overly worried, it did register as a unique experience and my level of concern was ramped up to "Level 5".

The following month, roughly four weeks after this disorientation, I awoke, got out of bed, got dressed, made it to the kitchen and collapsed on the floor. Nothing was broken, and I did manage to get up quite quickly. This did, however, set off alarm bells, for myself and my partner, and it was decided that another trip to the Emergency Room was in order. What ensued was an impressive journey through the Canadian Medical system. Over the next while I was assigned a Neurologist—Dr. Spacey (I kid you not)—and underwent a battery of tests...ECGs, EEGs, MRIs, scans, blood work and conversations with various specialists.

I was truly impressed with our Medical System and how thorough and attentive it could be—I felt quite adequately prodded and poked.

Despite all of this, my Neurologist wasn't able to come up with a conclusive diagnosis so I was forwarded to an Epileptologist—Dr. Hrazdil. While all of this medical attention and analysis was going on I continued to have these episodes once a month—like clockwork, from May through to December of 2012—but I didn't suffer another collapse until my final seizure in late December. Throughout this eight-month period of sobriety and seizures, I was more curious than concerned. I had faith in my specialists and was able to witness my episodes more as an observer than a patient. Overall, I found the experiences interesting.

In December I was to see my Epileptologist for the last time. Dr H. was eight-plus months pregnant and getting ready for maternity leave and motherhood. Despite all the tests, she was uncertain as to the nature of my malady. She had spoken with her supervisor and he was aware of a rare condition called Transient Epileptic Amnesia (apparently, fewer than 100 people have been diagnosed with this condition worldwide) which seemed to fit my list of symptoms, but they weren't prepared to commit to a diagnosis, or prescribe anything as a remedy—just yet. The idea was to "keep an eye on it" and see how things played out. I mentioned to her my suspicion that it may have been predicated by my years of heavy drinking, and the similarity to the Alcohol Withdrawal Seizure I'd suffered in 2010...she remained opaque on this issue and would neither support nor deny it.

A few weeks after this final meeting with Dr. H., at the end of December, I had another seizure which resulted in a collapse (my final one)—in the exact same spot that I'd collapsed and broken my left foot in 2010—the only difference was...this time I broke three metatarsal bones in my left foot.

When you have seizures, collapse, and break things, the medical system fast-tracks you, and you move to the front of the queue for further specialist attention. Because my Epileptologist was off having a baby, I was plunked back in front of my Neurologist—Dr. Spacey—in rather short order, in early January...plastic cast, crutches, contrition and all.

God bless the internet....and Wikipedia. Having received the tentative diagnosis of Transient Epileptic Amnesia from my Epileptologist, I had done my homework and tracked down a bundle of info on Wikipedia, including; symptoms; diagnosis; epidemiology; and treatment etc...and, what finally convinced me that I indeed had TEA was this quote:

"The IQ of people diagnosed with Transient Epileptic Amnesia tends to be in the high average to superior range..."

"Yeah, that was it," I thought, "it wasn't the alcohol abuse, it was because I was *too smart!"* ...I immediately curtailed all excessive intelligence and limited my smart thinking to one day a week.

As I sat with my Neurologist in her office on that cold January morning she asked, "What did your Epileptologist say?"

"Well," I replied, "she thought it might be a rare condition, something called Transient Epileptic Amnesia."

"Really? Hmmm, I've never heard of that before," replied Dr. S.

"Well," I said, "There's a fair bit of info on Wikipedia."

"Hmm, OK, let me have a look," she said as she pulled out her laptop.

For a few minutes she was engrossed in reading about this new condition, and then inquired,

"Did Dr. Hrazdil prescribe anything for you?"

"No," I replied, "it was just a tentative diagnosis so no prescription was given."

"Well, let's see what it says on Wikipedia," she said.

Diving back into her laptop for a few minutes, with a few nods, "uh-huh's" and the occasional raised eyebrow she finally said:

"Oh...OK...Carbamazepine...sure, that's a fairly well-known anti-seizure medication, I can prescribe that for you."

I must admit I was a little stunned...diagnosis to prescription within five minutes from Wikipedia! I was torn between the relief of having my condition diagnosed—with a prescribed remedy—and my inherent mistrust of any information gleaned from the net.

Ultimately, my fear of breaking further limbs overcame my mistrust of "diagnosis via internet" and I rushed out to fill my prescription.

Now, as I write this little story—10 years seizure-free—I am still in awe of the implications of the Wikipedia diagnosis. With fewer than 100 people worldwide diagnosed with this condition, the solution—or cure—would have been unlikely if not impossible in our pre-connected world...great things ahead for remote communities with limited medical facilities...and one more hurdle overcome on my personal journey of recovery.

I am grateful—one day at a time.

9

"I Could Tell You Wasn't a Roughneck"

The message coming out of Northern Alberta in the mid 1970s was a clarion call for young men such as Bill M. and myself. Everyone seemed to be talking about the "Big Money" being made in the Oil Sands north of Edmonton, and my friend Bill and I felt we were wasting our time slinging steak and lobster at The Keg in Richmond.

"I've heard of some guys making over $20 an hour," said Bill, "starting wages are like $7 or $8 but there's a lot of overtime."

"Time-and-a-half, and double-time," I said, "and I've heard that once you get in with a drilling company you can move up pretty quickly."

"And, if you're good and stick with it, you can get in with better companies paying more money," said Bill.

We both paused, and salivated a bit over the prospect of "Big Money" before we took another sip of our beers.

Our Friday night shift at The Keg was over. All the cocktail girls and waiters had cashed out and were sitting around drinking, chatting and listening to Morris and Wetback (as he liked to be known) play guitar and sing. It wasn't enough that Bill and I made decent money (with our wages and tips) surrounded by affable college-bound co-workers, in a warm, clean, safe and fun environment—no—our perceptions were being obscured by the overpowering lure of Big Money working in the oil-patch.

"My cousin is working on a rig and he made enough to hitchhike around Europe for a year," said Sue P., one of my favourite cocktail waitresses, and unfortunately, Morris's girlfriend.

"A buddy of mine just got back from Fort McMurray after 4 months as a Roughneck and made enough to buy a Camaro and pay for a year's tuition at UBC", said Higgs, taking a big gulp from his Harvey Wallbanger.

For Bill and I these additional stories added fuel to the fire of our 20-something, young male dreams of cash, cars and holidays.

"Maybe we could earn enough to pay for a university education so we can become professionals and not have to work as waiters or Roughnecks," I said.

Bill pondered my comment for a moment, took another swig of his beer and said, with a slightly inebriated smile on his face, "Naaah, that's crazy dude…think of all that cash—we're talking Big Money working on a rig…dream a little Georgie—maybe get outta that basement suite, rent a bigger apartment and ditch that crappy stereo you have for a new Kenwood… babes like a guy with money."

Large carbon footprints, were not yet looked upon with disdain.

I knew Bill and I were on different life trajectories, but he spoke a mean game—I was sold on the idea. Without even really knowing what a Roughneck was, or did, two soft-handed urban dreamers from Vancouver, decided to go and find out.

In fairly short order, we quit our jobs, gave notice on our living arrangements, said goodbye to friends and family, stuffed some clothes and a toothbrush into a couple of backpacks, threw them—and a dozen cans of beer, or "road pops" as they were called—onto the back seat of my '68 Volkswagen Station Wagon, and we were off.

Edmonton was our destination, where both Bill and I had family to stay with while we began our job search—calling up drilling companies out of the yellow pages that would hire untrained workers.

How hard could "Roughnecking" be, we thought. We'd both had post-high school labourer type jobs in construction, pulp mills, logging camps and fish boats. We imagined that this would be a variation on a theme—resource extraction, another notable Canadian pastime as "hewers of wood and drawers of water". Heavy physical labour with small groups of like-minded young men, good wages and benefits, sleeping and eating in bunkhouses away from civilization, with the constant threat of death or dismemberment lurking among the machinery.

Before the Coquihalla connector was built our fastest option was a 1300 kilometre trip to Edmonton on the Trans-Canada Highway—which we divided into two days with an overnight camping stop in Banff. Once you get beyond Hope, the scenery improves immensely, and we chose the Fraser Canyon through Spuzzum, Hell's Gate, and Kamloops into Thompson Country. Then on to Salmon Arm, Sicamous and Revelstoke on our way through the Kootenay-Columbia District, and the Rockies into Banff.

Under normal circumstances, we would've turned this road trip through paradise into an open-ended journey of adventure, discovery and fun—camping, drinking beer, getting high and trying to meet girls. But we were on a mission, and seemed unusually fixated (unusual for me at least, maybe Bill wasn't cursed with my easily-distracted Butterfly Brain) on getting to the oil patch, finding jobs and making money.

"Let's keep our eyes on the prize," said Bill, "once me make Big Bucks in Alberta, we can come back here and do it up in style."

The trip from Banff to Edmonton the following day was relatively uneventful—once we hit Calgary, we turned north on Highway 2, readjusting to the big vistas and long straight highways of Prairie travel now that we had exited the mountains and foothills. We travelled in short order through Red Deer, passing Ponoka and Wetaskiwin enroute to Edmonton.

My uncle Carl and aunt Roberta—who lived in Sherwood Park, on the Eastern outskirts of Edmonton—had kindly offered to put me up for as long as it took to find work, but my first order of business was to drop Bill off at his cousin's place in Garneau, an area of Edmonton just south of the Saskatchewan River.

"We made it man," I said, "got here in one piece" "Hard to say how long it's going to take to find a job, but I'll probably start calling around tomorrow, after I visit with my relatives tonight, how about you?"

"Yeah, I don't want to hang around my cousins any longer than I have to, I'll start job-hunting tomorrow," he replied, "Here's Gary's phone number…let me know how you're doing."

"Likewise," I said, "you've got my uncles number but let's check in…who knows, maybe we'll get a job on the same rig."

"Ha Ha!", that would be great," said Bill, "unlikely…but great…I'd probably move up the ladder faster than you and become your boss," he continued."

"Great," I said, "then you could promote me."

We both laughed as I pulled up to the curb outside Gary's place. Bill grabbed his bag from the back seat and popped out of the car.

"Good luck man…stay safe," he said.

"You too bro'," I replied.

We shook hands and he turned and left—I never saw him again.*

After two days on the road, a big family meal and lively conversation with Carl and Roberta and my young cousins, I was ready to hit the sack.

"I think I'm going to call it a night," I said, "gotta get up early tomorrow to start calling around."

"Whatever you need to do," said Roberta, "our home is your home, take as much time as you need…I wish we had contacts in the industry that we could give you but we don't—we do know that they're hiring right now and there are lots of jobs."

"That's good to hear, thanks a lot guys," I said, "I really appreciate your hospitality—good night."

After coffee and a hearty breakfast the next morning, I grabbed the telephone, pen and paper, and the Yellow Pages, and sat at the kitchen table, in order to start calling Drilling companies, getting names, and making notes. In what I thought would be an arduous, week-long search for employment. The first company I called was Gunnarson Drilling and the conversation went something like this:

"Hi my name's George, I'm looking for work as a Roughneck, are you guys hiring?"

"Yup sure are, have you ever worked as a Roughneck?"

"Yes, I have," I lied.

"Great, when can you start?"

"Immediately," I replied.

"Have you got a car?", he asked.

"Yeah, I'm driving a blue Volkswagen Station Wagon."

"Ok, go to the corner of Jasper Avenue and 106th Street at 7:00 a.m. tomorrow—heading west—and one of our trucks will meet you there. It's a dark brown GMC truck with Gunnarson Drilling on the door. Mike will be driving…he'll wave at you when he sees you. You're going to follow him to the drill site—about three hours west of Edmonton past Whitecourt…make sure you've got gas."

And that was it…I had a job.

I spent the rest of the day getting ready for this unexpected escalation of opportunity. I'd never been hired—sight unseen—before, so had to make sure I was as prepared as my limited knowledge of the job would allow.

"Hmm…dirty yellow coveralls, hard hat and Dayton work boots from my logging camp days…socks, underwear, pants, shirts, harmonicas…yeah, all set."

I called Bill to let him know that I'd landed work. He hadn't started his own search yet and was a bit surprised by my speedy hiring.

"That's wild man, and you haven't even met these guys yet," he said, "what about paperwork? Not even a job application?"

"The guy on the phone said that the guy in the truck would have a form for me to fill out," I replied, "You should give these guys a call, maybe they need more workers."

He wrote down the name of the company.

"I'll try them tomorrow, thanks for the lead…good luck bro' gotta run the cousin's here."

"You too man," I said, "take me for a ride in your Lamborghini when I see you in Vancouver!"

We both laughed and hung up the phones—I never talked to him again.*

Carl and Roberta were also surprised (and likely secretly relieved) that I'd landed work so quickly.

"I knew the oil patch was hot, but I've never seen hiring in action—sight unseen and over the phone—that's incredible," said Carl, as we sat having an unexpected final meal together before I left for the rigs. "And, you just meet these guys, in their truck, at a corner downtown…and wave to each other?" he asked incredulously.

"Yeah," I replied, "I know it sounds weird, but I'll probably run over and introduce myself, before I follow them into the Alberta wilderness…I guess they needed to know if I'd be riding in the truck or following in my own vehicle." And then, as an afterthought, "Maybe you guys should write down the name of the company in case I die or go missing."

"Oh George," groaned Roberta, rolling her eyes, "that's not very comforting, I hope you're just kidding."

"Don't worry guys, I'm just pulling your leg," I said laughing, "I'll be just fine, but I do think you should have the company name, here, I've written it down."

"And I'm not sure if it was a good idea to lie about your work experience," said Roberta, "they might expect you to hit the ground running."

"Not to worry guys," I said cockily, "I've had introductory labor type jobs before and you pretty much learn everything by noon on the first day and then just repeat that …or fake it til you make it, as they say…and I think hiring a guy over the phone shows they don't expect much."

"Hmmm, maybe…," said Roberta, "…hey, why don't we have a look at your repetitive work skills in action," she continued, "…you can give us a hand with these dishes again tonight."

We all laughed, and rose to clear the table.

I arrived at the appointed meeting place in good time the next morning, parked and waited for Mike. As planned, a dirty, well-used, late model GMC Truck, with assorted oil patch related gear piled in the cargo bed, pulled up beside me around 7:00 a.m., and a bearded 30-ish guy opened his window and said, "Hey, are you George?"

"Yes," I replied.

"Nice to meet you…I'm Mike, just keep following my truck until we get to the drilling site parking area, it's about a 3-hour drive west of here along Highway 43…are you all gassed up?"

"Sure am," I nodded again. And we were off.

We followed the Yellowhead Highway west for about an hour before hanging a right at Manly Corner when we hit the 43. The region is a checkerboard of large farms and flat prairie scrubland before it transitions into pine forest dotted with stands of Trembling Aspen and Balsam Poplar. By the time we hit Whitecourt and crossed the Athabasca River we'd left the better part of the farmland behind and were into a region of active drilling, extraction and exploration.

Somewhere between Two Creeks, and Fox Creek—essentially, in the middle of nowhere—Mike hung a sharp right onto a muddy unpaved single lane road and headed north into the bush. I followed as best I could, bumping and swerving in the rutted tracks until we hit a clearing which was used as a parking and staging area. Mike stopped in the middle of the parking area and motioned for me to park my car off to the side, gather my gear and hop into the truck with him for the final leg of the trip.

I'm a fairly affable guy, some might even say "chatty" but I could tell from Mike's more taciturn demeanor that bubbly conversation was not in the cards.

"How much further to the rig?", I asked.

"About another mile or so…your Volkswagen wouldn't've made it…it gets pretty boggy," he said, as he gunned the engine and carried on down the road.

"Jesus, I thought, how much worse can this road get?"

It didn't take long to find out. They'd had a heavy rain the night before and the road ahead– after we left the parking area—looked like a stream. Mike did the best he could, swerving, navigating and avoiding the worst of the sucking bog and giant puddles, but eventually the spinning of the tires and lack of forward movement let us know we were stuck.

"Shit," said Mike, "it's gotten a hell of a lot worse since I was here four days ago…oh well." Without missing a beat, he reached for his walkie talkie. "Anybody there?"… crackle, crackle… "Hello! Dave!...you there?" And, in fairly short order,

"Hey…Mike is that you? Where are ya?"

"I'm in a company truck with the new guy, stuck in the mud about halfway to the site…can you come and get us?"

"Uhh sure," replied Dave ... crackle, crackle… "I'll fire up the Caterpillar and see you in about 20."

We hopped back in the truck waiting to be rescued. I shared a bit of small talk with Mike and we exchanged basic info about ourselves while we waited. Where we were from (he was from Newfoundland), what his position was on the rig (he was a Motorman—responsible for engine maintenance), and how long he'd been working in the fields. He'd started as a Roughneck five years earlier and had worked his way up….and showed no sign of surprise when I told him I was brand new to rig work.

"Well," he said, "I started the same as you…you gotta start somewhere, they don't send you to Roughneck school…it's pretty basic work, you'll catch on…just try not to get injured."

Good advice I thought, but not exactly comforting.

Before long a big yellow dozer came slowly but surely down the road towards us, grinding away and belching diesel, and seemingly oblivious to the four-wheel-drive crippling conditions upon which it travelled effortlessly. Upon arrival, Dave hopped off the Cat, teased Mike for getting stuck, shook my hand in greeting, then released the winch, and let out enough wire to secure the front of our truck and drag us back to camp.

There was no rest for the road-weary. Once we arrived in camp, we parked the truck, I was shown to my bunk in a four-man trailer to drop off my stuff, and then followed Mike to the cookhouse trailer to grab a bite of lunch and meet the other crew before I started my shift.

Dave who towed us into camp was another roughneck and was already face deep into a bowl of chili, as was Leasehand Andy—or handy Andy—as he was known. Mike was already eating at the communal table, deep in conversation with Derrickhand Steve. I sat with my plastic tray loaded with basic camp food and slowly familiarized with the others I'd be working with.

"The Rig Manager doesn't join us too often, he seems to like his peace and quiet," said Dave.

"Which is kinda crazy when you work on a noisy oil rig that operates 24/7," countered Mike, "Anyone seen Brandon?"

Brandon, the Tool Push, or Driller as they are now known, was the crew's boss, who worked under the supervision of the Rig Manager. Just as the crew speculated on his whereabouts—which included mostly vulgar observations about Brandon's bodily functions—a wiry hawk-faced man in his late 30s opened the door, scanned the room quickly and, gesturing at me, said,

"You…new guy…when you're done eating come and meet me on the platform."

Not the friendliest of introductions to one's boss, but not out of my realm of experience. It's not atypical for niceties to be pared down or eliminated altogether in these "all male" labouring gigs where entry level positions see a pretty high turnover rate, and, as I discovered over lunch, my predecessor, a young guy from Timmins, had just lost four of his upper front teeth in a rig accident when a length of pipe bucked up and knocked them out a few days prior.

My meeting with Brandon was short and to the point.

"Ok, new guy…I'm Brandon and I'll be your boss on this rig, you told head office that you've worked on the rigs before…," he said, looking at me with a mix of skepticism and disdain, "because you're low man on the totem pole—as long as you can follow instructions from everyone else, even the other roughnecks, you'll probably do OK. For now, I want you to join Andy and Dave hauling mud up to the tank, they'll show you where we keep it." ("Mud" was a slang term for the 80-pound bags of powdered lubricant which were poured into a giant slurry vat and fed into the hole in the earth created by the drilling pipes—acting as a lubricant for the drilling.)

As I was soon to discover, Roughneck work alternated between strenuous heavy labour—carrying around 80-pound sacks of mud—

tedious low-maintenance cleaning of "the machine", and nerve-wracking, dangerous episodes where the entire crew sprang into action to change lengths of pipe. Dirty dangerous work with slippery mud belching onto the platform while giant clamps and chains were used to unscrew the existing pipe and attach new lengths….and then, repeat this sequence until lunch, dinner or coffee breaks gave welcome respite on the 12- or 16-hour shifts.

And why not work for 16 hours? We were so far away from civilization that there was nowhere to go, and nothing to do, except drink—a pastime that I was already quite good at.

Sleep, eat, work, drink…in the mid 70s, in the wilderness, these four words would define the life of an oil rig worker. Maybe it was just the promise of "Big Money" that kept a lot of men going. As there were no cell phones, internet, or television, it wasn't the lure of entertainment or intellectual stimulation. If you were lucky, you made a friend or two. I didn't stay long enough to find out.

A few aches and pains greeted me upon rising, but I was young and undaunted. The crew and I got up, ate breakfast and headed for the platform.

The oil rig is a machine, like a giant car engine, whose sole function is to drill into the earth and push lengths of pipe deeper and deeper through dirt and clay and rock—hundreds or thousands of feet—until oil is struck, and we, the crew, were there to perform our repetitive tasks until that primary mission was accomplished. Perhaps it was this numbing mindlessness that led my fellow roughnecks to seek distraction and entertainment through mischievous pranks. Handy Andy and Dave could tell—almost instinctively—when I met them in them in the cookhouse the day before, that I wasn't a seasoned hand at rig work, and was, therefore, an obvious target for their introductory hazing.

The three of us descended from the main platform, and headed for the palettes of Powdered Lubricant Mud to begin our work for the day—each grabbing an 80-pound bag of the stuff, lifting it up to our shoulders and carrying it over to the giant cauldron of bubbling mud, where we would pull out our Exacto knives, cut off an end, and dump the fine mixture into the tank to create a perfect lubricant slurry. After repeating this procedure two or three times, Dave and Andy stopped beside the palette and Andy said, "Dave, can you do this?", whereupon he lifted a sack of mud and slowly struggled to raise it over his head in a display of strength and male bravado, before dropping it with a thud back onto the palette. "Piece of cake," said Dave, as I stood nearby, watching their antics. Dave grabbed a bag and slowly, grunting and grimacing, raised the 80-pound sack until his arms were outstretched over his head in triumph, before he too chucked it back onto the palette.

"How about you Bathgate?", said Andy, "why don't-cha show us what Vancouver boys are made of."

I know how these male prowess challenges work. The gauntlet was thrown and it would've been unthinkable for me to decline the invitation, without risk of alienating my new work mates. Participation meant bonding, saying no meant looking like a poor sport, or worse—a fearful weakling. I grabbed a bag.

Looking directly at Andy, who'd started the game and issued the challenge, I put all of my energy and effort into doing "the lift" in two stages, stage one was raising the bag to my chest level and stage two was doing a modified version of a weightlifters clean and jerk motion, dropping slightly, spreading and planting my legs firmly and then using the biceps, triceps and pecs to complete the lift. Although I wasn't a fearful weakling, hefting an 80-pound bag over my head—when my total body weight was likely under 130 pounds—was a little out of my physical comfort zone. Slowly, I inched the bag to my reddened grimacing face, and then grunted and gasped as the bag ascended past my forehead, trembling and quivering as I gave it 'everything I had' to raise it up, to extended arm height over my head. At that very moment—almost imperceptibly—I heard the sound of Dave's Exacto Knife opening up behind me.

In my focused preoccupation lifting the bag, I'd forgotten about Dave, who had manoeuvred himself directly behind me, waiting for the perfect moment of bag apogee and victim distraction. With open blade he reached up and slit the bag completely in half releasing its powdery contents above my unwitting head. Eighty pounds of fine clay powder began cascading down over my head and body. Luckily my youthful reaction time was better than my dead-lift strength and I threw the bag to the side, avoiding the worst of this slapstick clown moment. My hardhat and the left side of my body bore the brunt of Andy and Dave's goofy hi-jinks.

Rule Number 2 of male hazing rituals—unless you've lost an eye or an appendage, don't get angry, take it as good-natured ribbing—the prank is not rejection, it is a test.

"Hahaha!", I laughed, "Nice one…do you do that with all the

new guys?".

Realizing that I wasn't about to attack them with my own Exacto knife, or rat them out to Brandon, they too laughed,

"Hahahaha!"...you got lucky dude!", said Dave, "some of the new guys get so covered in this shit they have to go take a shower,"... "powder's so fine it can stay in your clothes for weeks!", said Andy.

"Anyways boys, that's enough fun for now," said Dave, "we gotta keep hauling this stuff or Brandon will rag on us."

And then, we were back to work like nothing happened—situation normal—unless I detected a slight warming in my relationship with these two goofs.

Day 3...up at 7, shower, eat breakfast, engage in small talk or, for those nursing hangovers, grunt accordingly and drink lots of coffee. Because I was unaware that alcohol—and drugs—were the sole form of entertainment on the rigs, I didn't bring an adequate stash of my own, and was—therefore—spared the hangovers typical of my excessive nature. This clarity may have saved life and limb as I learned my duties and responsibilities on the job. My other crew mates were fairly generous and wouldn't begrudge me swigs of their whiskey as we sat around in our trailers after our shifts were over—I told them I'd pay them back whenever I made it back to the nearest town to stock up during the next rotation—when our three-week shift ended and we got our week off.

In addition to breakfast, lunch and dinner breaks—rig workers also received three 15-minute breaks per 12-hour shift, or four for 16 hours, and these breaks were often taken in a small bunkhouse on the platform to—briefly—escape the heat and clouds of mosquitos in summer, or the biting cold of winter. Usually, a thermos of lukewarm coffee and Styrofoam cups would be waiting there, and, not infrequently, a bottle of whiskey—depending on the predilections of the Tool Push or Rig Manager. Ours had both.

After putting in a solid half day of mind-deadening, backbreaking grunt work, I decided to head to the bunkhouse for my afternoon coffee. Andy and Dave were nowhere in sight so I assumed I'd find them there—my new best friends. I was half covered in a spew of drying mud that had belched upon me during the last pipe change. I was slowly learning where to position myself during the change to avoid this particular outcome but had miscalculated and had paid—once again—for my lack of experience.

As I entered the bunkhouse "the boys" looked up from their coffees, smiled, and Andy said, "Hey man, c'mon in…you should try a little whiskey in your coffee, Bob's left his bottle here for us to share." It didn't take much convincing for me to lively up my coffee so I grabbed the bottle of rye off the shelf and added a stiff two fingers to my half cup of joe and spoonful of Coffee Mate creamer. I sat on the bench, leaned against the wall, sipped my drink, closed my eyes for a moment and said,

"Mmm-mm, that's pretty good…good idea."

"And, Dude," said Dave, "when we're changing pipe you gotta jump back more when it's being released or you'll keep getting covered in mud."

"Yeah, thanks man," I replied, "that shit can really squirt out everywhere…don't worry I'll figure it out."

"Hey Dave," said Andy, "Do ya wanna play 'Cuttin' Rope' while we're hangin' out?"

"Yeah sure," said Dave, "we've got another 5 or 10 to kill…you got a rope?"

"Yeah, there's one over here below the bench," replied Andy, "why don't you grab the axe?"

Dave got up from the bench we shared, walked over to the adjacent wall and lifted the fire axe from its hooks, and sat back down. I sat quietly sipping my drink, watching with vague interest.

"We can use this as a blindfold," said Andy, as Dave put the axe down and affixed the piece of cloth over his eyes.

"OK, take off your hardhat, and I'll position the rope," said Andy, as he laid the rope on the floor a few feet in front of where Dave sat. Dave complied and picked up the axe. Now they had my attention…booze, an axe and a blindfold—what could go wrong?

As Dave held the axe in front of him, Andy grabbed the head of the axe and positioned it right above the rope and touched the axe blade to the rope.

"OK, there it is," said Andy, "you feel that?"

"Yup, I think so," said Dave.

"OK, give it your best shot!", Andy encouraged him.

Dave touched the axe blade to the rope several times to get his bearing and then lifted the axe over his head and brought it down forcefully with a resounding CHOP! …cutting halfway through the rope but not, completely chopping it in two which—I assumed—was the purpose of this, 'Fun for the Whole Family' game.

"Not bad," said Andy, as Dave peaked under his blindfold, "let me have a try."

Dave and Andy exchanged places. Andy sat on the bench beside me, affixed the blindfold, and grabbed the axe which Dave—in turn—positioned above the rope, touching it to the rope as Andy had done for him.

"OK, there's the rope," he said, "You got it?"

"Yup," replied Andy, "better stand back."

Dave complied as Andy now raised the axe over his head and then he too brought it down with a mighty CHOP!...this time missing the rope altogether but leaving a nice axe head shaped scar in the plywood floor. Peeking under his blindfold Andy moaned, "Aww, shit...I missed it...give me another try." Blindfold repositioned, axe in hand, Dave set him up again and Andy swung his axe with even greater force, and CHOP! Once again he missed his mark.

Of course, as I sat watching this spectacle, with the whisky working its magic, I thought, "That doesn't look too difficult, how the heck did he miss? I bet I could do better than Andy."

"Ha Ha!", laughed Dave, "you didn't even touch the rope...hey George, do you wanna try?"

"Sure," I said, "doesn't look too hard—set me up."

"OK, you'll need to take off your hardhat to get a good swing on the axe."

I took off my hardhat and set it on the bench beside me, put on the blindfold, grabbed the axe from Andy, and let Dave guide my axe to the rope.

"OK...you feel where the rope is?" asked Dave.

"Yeah, I got this," I replied.

"Ok, just let me get outta the way before you take your swing."

I touched my axe to the rope one more time to get my bearing then slowly lifted the axe above my head—I was going to show these clowns and nail this silly game. After I got the axe to a sufficient height, with my arms extended to the correct length and fulcrum to cut that sucker clean in half, I swung with all my might, and CRUNCH! Came the sound of a large red Fire Axe chopping deeply into my work hardhat.

Even before I managed to get my blindfold off and survey the damage to my hardhat, I could hear the hysterical laughter of Andy and Dave.

"Hahahahah! Nice one man!" laughed Dave, "Clean through the

top, chop chop."

I peeked under the blindfold at my aluminum hardhat, pierced and impaled on the axe. How the hell did I not see this one coming? I thought… "Oh yeah … I was blindfolded in a room with two mischief monkeys drinking whiskey." While I was concentrating on my swing, Andy had deftly removed the rope and replaced it with my hat.

Hazing Ritual #2 successful…check.

"Jesus," I said as I checked out the damage and slowly wiggled the hardhat free from the grip of the axe, sticking a baby finger through the hole, "how many more of these fun games do you guys have?"

"Ha ha!" laughed Andy, "you should've seen your face when the axe went into your hat C-R-U-N-C-H," he embellished.

Just then, Tool Push Brandon opened the door, stuck his head in, and said, "OK morons, coffee break's over, c'mon, let's get back to work." Immediately subdued, Andy and Dave replied, "Sure thing Boss," in unison, and I just nodded, sticking my wounded hat back onto my head.

After Prank Number 2, my radar was up and I was fairly confident that "the boys" wouldn't be able to pull another fast one on me. We just carried on with our grinding jobs as I incrementally developed lift and carry muscles, and spotted the best position to be in for the pipe changes to avoid getting covered in mud. I'm a fairly quick learner, but I was already recognizing the drawbacks of working on the rigs. "Sure, the money's good," I thought, "but only because you have to work 12 and 16 hour days to get overtime, doing this crappy job, eating their shitty food …with guys you don't really like…while hearing stories about other guys getting injured on other rigs."

We'd just heard rumours of a nearby rig getting hit by lightning, injuring a couple of workers. "Great," I thought, "getting injured seems to be a real crap shoot, it's like a Bad Luck Lottery."

Day 4 broke overcast and warm. It was September in Northern Alberta and mosquitos were slowly being replaced by clouds of blackflies and stinging wasps. Breakfast, at least, was substantial, typical and hearty—as it was in most camps. Bacon or Ham and Eggs, toast, hash browns, Orange Juice and a bottomless cup of coffee. I'd developed a coffee habit from my days hitchhiking across Canada at age 17, and staying at Youth Hostels where a pot of free coffee was always percolating—so this limitless access gave a heavily caffeinated start to my days.

Already the repetitive nature of the job was sinking in and I was getting the hang of what was expected of me. I met my "buddies" Andy and Dave on the platform and we proceeded with our duties with an occasional word or instruction from Brandon, or Bob the Rig Manager. We were so low on the totem pole that anyone else on the rig could ask us to do something—even the Derrickhand, or Motorman—and we'd have to comply. Thus far, most of the bossing had been reserved for the Driller, Brandon, a no-nonsense kind of guy who seemed largely devoid of humour, compassion, kindness, or interest in others—which really means he didn't seem interested in me, as I had no real idea how he got along with his own peers or superiors.

It was late morning and I found myself returning to the mud bag pile from the vat when Brandon appeared from somewhere within the machinery of the rig, and—in order to make himself heard—shouted,

"Hey, George!" (it was the first time he'd called me by my first name…up to this point it had been "Bathgate" or "New Guy") "I needja to do something…put whatever you're doing on hold and follow me."

Obediently I trailed behind him along a narrow corridor into the belly of the machine which powered the entire rig. I was no longer in tedious/repetitive territory—it was hot, deafening and unfamiliar…and somewhere I'd not yet been, seen, nor dreamed of. We came to a three rung metal ladder leading up to a narrow aperture onto a two-foot wide, 10-foot-long platform, claustrophobically encased by what appeared to be the very heart of the machine—an endlessly roaring beast, giving power and drive to the primary function—drill baby drill.

Brandon grabbed my arm, stood me in front of the small metal ladder, pointed into the opening of the gates of hell and shouted,

"Do you see that handle!?"

He was pointing to a small handle which appeared to be the only visible, movable thing on the far wall of the roaring dark nook—about a 10 or 12-foot crouch walk up the ladder and along the narrow platform.

"Yes!" I shouted back.

"I want you to go in there and turn that handle to the left."

Well, that seems pretty straightforward, I thought, and, without further adieu, I reached up, and curled my gloved fingers around the metal housing surrounding the aperture in order to pull myself up. My left hand was immediately stung by an incredibly fast and forceful ZING! Running across all my fingers, startling me, and causing me to instinctively pull my hand back and hold it protectively to my chest. I didn't know if I was in pain or shock.

"Take off your glove!" Brandon shouted.

I looked up slightly bewildered.

"Your glove..TAKE IT OFF!" he shouted again with emphasis.

I took the glove off, to show him that none of my fingers had been cut off inside the glove.

"OK…you're fine…put your glove back on …pull yourself up with those rungs." He pointed at two hand rungs positioned especially for that purpose. Gingerly, carefully, I crawled into the cavity, reached the handle, turned it to the left and crawled back out.

When we exited the machine to the open air of the platform, where the deafening noise abated—somewhat—Brandon said, "You stuck your hand into the housing for the 10-foot fans that cool off the machine…be more careful…I've seen guys lose fingers." Then he turned and headed back to whatever he was doing before our encounter.

There was a definite groove on my leather work gloves where the fan had whizzed across my fingers. I stood for a few moments reflecting on the significance of what had just happened before returning to work. Sweet, I thought, with a soupçon of sangfroid, I could've just lost my fingers…how much are these fingers worth? Big Money? Or are they priceless?

"Hey man!" shouted Andy, as he came up from the mud bag palettes, "there you are…we'd wondered where you'd gone…c'mon it's time to change some pipe." My dark reverie interrupted, I turned and followed Andy up the catwalk to the drilling platform.

I was feeling a little off my game, realizing that my cocky "How hard could it be" approach to the job of Roughneck really didn't factor in risk of serious injury. I elected to forego the 16-hour shift, in favour of the shorter 12-hour day so I could get off at 8, mull over my situation…and spend a few quality hours at night with the other louts swigging whisky from a 26-er while ogling the Penthouse centerfolds Mike had taped up on the walls around his bunk. Foremost on my mind was picking their more seasoned brains on the topic of "work related injuries"—who better to ask?

It didn't take long to loosen up their tongues, they all had stories to tell and were willing—let's say eager—to share increasingly gruesome incidents, both personal and anecdotal. When I mentioned my brush with near digit removal, Mike laughed and held up his hand which was missing half a baby finger.

"I lost this the same way as you on the first rig I worked on…fuckin' driller could've warned me," he said.

Then Andy piped up, "I broke my ankle slipping on the catwalk while carrying a bag of mud…gave me a nice little six-week EI holiday."

"Yeah, I cracked three ribs on my left side when one of the clamps bucked back during a pipe change…God it was painful to breathe," said Dave, "I was off for about a month with that one."

"I've seen guys get whipped when the chains break while they're throwin' the chains.", said Mike, "or having a foot crushed by a length of pipe if it slips," he continued. "Moving the rig is pretty dangerous too…once ya hit oil ya gotta cap it off and take the whole rig apart and move it somewhere else…and then set it up—that's pretty shitty work."

Jesus, I thought, it's not "if", it's "when" I get injured…and Mike's observation that the Driller could've warned him and saved his finger stuck with me. Brandon could've done the same thing with me but was either testing me… or, just playing with me. I felt a bit disposable—working with guys and a boss who either didn't care or actively disliked me. And the idea of disassembling this entire operation, packing it up and moving it just seemed too unappealing to contemplate.

There were whole layers of this job that just sucked—except for the "Big Money"—which, I now envisioned, enjoying in my new motorized wheelchair with my prosthetic arm and eye patch.

"Guys, I gotta hit the sack," I said, as I got up to leave for my trailer, "oh, and thanks for the shots of CC…I owe you."

I rose the next morning, invigorated, despite my semi-sleepless night of rumination. A little bacon and eggs and coffee seemed like the best plan as I knew it was going to be a long day. My mischievous mates joined me and we ate and joked as the morning sun poured through the small windows of the Kitchen Trailer. We finished, got up and returned our trays to the stainless-steel counter before heading out the door to begin our shifts. As the boys headed for the platform, I said,

"I'll catch up with you guys later…just gotta see Brandon first," as I veered towards his office.

I knocked, and Brandon said, "Come in." I poked my head in the door…he didn't seem too surprised to see me. "What's up?" he asked.

I entered the Office Trailer where he and the Rig Manager both had desks, and sat in the chair nearest to him, looked him in the eyes and said, "I quit." He held my gaze for a moment, expressionless, and said, "OK…get your gear from your bunk, and meet me at the truck."

I didn't bother to say any other goodbyes…what was the point? I'd made a decision, and the clarity of purpose and certainty felt good—I'd decided to terminate my 4-day career as a roughneck and head back to the coast. I stuffed everything into my backpack and headed for the parking lot. Brandon was already there with the truck running, so I threw my pack in the back and hopped into the cab beside him. We were both silent for the short 10-minute drive to where I'd left my car—luckily several dry days allowed the truck to make the trip without the assistance of a caterpillar.

As we stopped in the cleared staging/parking area, Brandon turned to me before I got out of the truck and said, sarcastically,

"I could tell you wasn't a Roughneck."

I turned to look at him for a moment, "It's weren't," I said derisively, and got out of the truck, glad to see that my Volkswagen hadn't been vandalized in this remote wasteland. I pulled my gear from the cargo bed, looked up at the sun peeking through the fleecy white clouds, and feeling as free as a bird.

Epilogue:

And my friend Bill? These were the days without internet, Cell phones, and social media. When we said goodbye, our lives really did take separate turns, and we had little, or no way of remaining in touch. We didn't know each other's families, we had no addresses or phone numbers beyond the two we exchanged in Edmonton, and, like many young men, became so busy and engaged with our lives that reconnecting was not necessary nor a priority.

I heard from a mutual friend when I returned to Vancouver, that Bill had found a job on a rig and—unlike myself—had stuck with it and may have chosen to continue working in "the patch".

I heard he made "Big Money".

10

The Armed Robbery

These days, I feel like writing and seem to enjoy it when I do so. As the larger writing projects, have—thus far—eluded me, I've been "warming up" with some short stories—primarily personal anecdotes from the now distant past, or, journal-like entries from recent experience. Recent experience could include a story called "My Life in Coffee Shops" as this truly has become my preferred location for all of my writing activity and is where I am now...comfortably ensconced at a table surrounded by "the buzz" of a little grocery store/coffee shop hybrid called BeFresh, in Kitsilano. A store, not unlike the Herb and Spice Shop on Bank Street in Ottawa, where I apprehended an armed robber in the early 80s.

 I don't recall exactly where I was headed, but it was a Friday night, I was in my mid-20s, and I was walking north on Bank Street, in Ottawa, without a care in the world. I was, in all likelihood, going to a friend's place, en route to a pub, to try and meet girls.

 The Herb and Spice Shop was our neighbourhood grocery store. This was the owner's second location after his flagship store in the Glebe proved profitable. It was nearby and it was friendly, and I'd developed a first-name relationship with the staff. On this night, the sweet and bright Debbie T. was running the store and getting ready to close up to follow her own, youthful, Friday night pursuits.

 As I approached the Herb and Spice, engrossed in my own plans for the evening, Debbie burst out the front door onto the sidewalk, scuffling with a rough-looking unshaven man in his mid to late 30s. In the midst of their frantic dance, he pushed her to the sidewalk and ran north on Bank—clutching a handful of money.

 "Stop that guy! He's stolen our money," she shouted.

 I think a heroic act must involve some thought of the possible consequences of one's actions—a conscious decision to act, despite foreknowledge that a threatening situation may contain risk of harm to self. That, is heroic and admirable. Often though, in the face of danger, when our reptilian brain is offering only limited choice: Door #1, labelled "Fight" or Door #2, labelled "Flight", we do not always have the metered luxury of thought. When friends or loved one's are in peril, the rush of adrenaline shakes Mr. Lizard awake with the stark choice: "Are you going to run away, or are you going to step in? Feeling lucky? ... Punk?"

A small group, of maybe 2 or 3 individuals, who were slightly closer to the mayhem than I, gave chase. "Aaah…those three should be able to get that guy," I thought, as my lizard slowly slunk back into its reptilian lair.

"But this is exciting,"…"And I like Debbie,"…"And perhaps I can help,"…"Safety in numbers,"…"Maybe I'll get free groceries," … "And it's on my way," I thought, all in a nanosecond. So, I joined the pack, in hot pursuit of our prey—the evil-doer.

Not far from the Herb and Spice Store, on the next corner, was a bar, which I did not frequent. I was a Royal Oak guy with its lovely faux British pub feel (and Kilkenny on tap) so I had little reason to go to this watering hole, which catered to career alcoholics and the country music crowd. (I, and my friends, were—of course—too cool for that with our New Wave hair and obsessions). I don't know what possessed the stick-up guy to enter this bar as a means to escape his pursuers but he did so by way of the side door—slipping into the dinghy, smoky, and noisy pub interior in a frantic bid for freedom. The three closest pursuers, who were hot on his trail, followed him doggedly into the bar, and I arrived, moments later, slightly out of breath as the Pub door closed.

"Those guys are bound to catch him inside the Pub," I reasoned, "and, therefore, don't need me to add to the pandemonium"…"I'd just get in the way", "He's probably already caught", "I might unwittingly discover I like country music"…"Hmmm…I have an idea," I thought, "I'll go stand by the front door in case they don't catch him—which is highly unlikely—and stop him there if he emerges, also, highly unlikely."

I strategically repositioned myself to the front door of the pub…and waited.

I didn't have to wait long, and it wasn't long enough to form any kind of coherent plan. The three pursuers had failed in their simple mission—catch the bad guy—and suddenly, here he was, bursting out of the pub, wild-eyed and breathless and clutching a handful of money. Mr. Lizard was abruptly and rudely awoken from his complacent slumber.

"Fight or flight Georgie? What's it going to be? C'mon…you've got…uh… less than a second to decide."

I pulled my right arm back, made an unaccustomed fist and punched the hold-up man squarely in the face.

Up to this point in life, I'd never really had that all too-common male experience of beating someone up. I was a skinny bespectacled New Wavish kinda guy and this was the first time I'd struck somebody with force and intent in the face. My fleeting thought, for it wasn't a plan, was that the criminal should somehow, easily and readily, succumb to my punches and crumple to the ground…unconscious. I just…wanted…to knock …him out.

"Not so quickly my effete friend," spoke Mr. Reality, "The gentleman you've just assaulted has been in worse scuffles and received far more damaging blows from a life of petty crime and stints in the penal system. Your pitiful attempt at "punching" is likely just going to remind him of the injustices he suffered at the hands of a cruel father and will only serve to enrage him." Stunned momentarily, Mr. Criminal leapt at me and grabbed my coat with his one free hand. We scuffled upright briefly but his unwillingness to let go of the cash and my height advantage gave me enough leverage to throw him to the ground, sit on his chest and punch him again—with the greater force of my now seasoned experience—directly in the face…twice.

While our scuffle was taking place, several things happened: the original pursuers exited the bar and now surrounded us as non-participatory onlookers, quite likely thinking, "Oh good…the skinny guy has him pinned…looks like he's got it covered...what a great puncher…let's just watch"; Debbie appeared out of the now-gathering crowd and grabbed the cash from the perps hand…freeing him up to fight back more effectively—which he did, and; a bunch of drunks, who had no idea what was actually going on spilled out of the bar and surrounded us while we fought.

"Hey," said one of the Waylon and Willie listening bar patrons in his familiar beer-soaked slur, "Stop yer fightin'…get off that guy,"

While "Mama's Don't Letcher Babies Grow up ta be Cowboys", emanated from the bar, several sets of nicotine-stained hands reached down, grabbed me roughly from behind and pulled me away from "the guy".

Pandemonium ensued as the original pursuers protested fruitlessly, Debbie shouted something inaudibly, and I stammered ineffectively to the alcoholic liberators. There was nary a hint of understanding or sympathy in their rheumy eyes—perhaps the robber was their friend and the stolen loot was intended to buy rounds of beer at the pub. Recognizing an opportunity, and, without missing a beat, our street-smart hoodlum got up, glanced furtively around, and chose—unwisely—to run back into the bar through the open front door.

Like bloodhounds, back in the chase, the original pursuers took off after their prey and ran into the bar in hot pursuit. The drunks, sensing that something exciting was unfolding, and likely feeling thirsty after all their strenuous activity poured themselves back into the bar to order more beer and obstruct justice. Debbie had disappeared, likely to return the $$ and get on with her evening, now that her role in this drama was over, and I, once again in very short order, found myself alone outside the pub as events were unfolding inside.

"They're bound to catch him this time," I thought, "no need for me to go in there…it's a done deal…how could they miss him this time? That'd be crazy,"…"But…if they do," I thought, "I might as well go and stand guard by the back door as a highly unlikely and unnecessary, back-up plan."

I walked around to the side door and waited…again. I didn't have to wait long.

I'm not sure if it was fear or surprise that I saw in his eyes when he burst, once again, out of the pub through the side door, but his internal Reptile was definitely giving him the "flight" command. His brief startled pause, and the dismay of recognition made him attempt an evasive action but it was of no use. Once again, lacking any grand strategy or experience in the apprehension of evil-doers, I pulled my arm back, made a fist, and punched him square in the face. I was a one-trick pony who just wanted his opponent to succumb to the simple knock-out punch.

Panicky and enraged, and definitely not unconscious, he reached for my lapels while I put my violent Plan B into effect. "Perhaps if I just grab his head and repeatedly bash it against the brick wall he'll crumple and I can sit on him until the police come…they will come—won't they?"

Plan B, on a determined, wily, motivated opponent was not having the desired effect. After four or five vigorous headsmashings, he broke free of my grip and ran towards a cab, which had just pulled over to the curb to see what was going on. "Get me out of here!!" he shouted, to the bewildered cabbie, as he flung open the back door and threw himself into the cab.

I'm not sure, exactly, what script I was following then. It was all so primal, without a whiff of rationality or forethought. I was in the fight and was somehow still protecting my friend Debbie and my neighbourhood. Perhaps internal codes of conduct—good versus evil—were playing out and directing my actions in this little street drama. Maybe I was just a young male jacked up on adrenaline and testosterone.

I reached into the cab, hauled my victim out, threw him to the ground, sat on his chest and punched him forcibly in the face. "Stop struggling or I'll keep hitting you," I said…."Where are those fucking police?", I thought. Fearfully, eyes darting and weighing his options, he finally chose capitulation over struggle. I'm not sure who was most relieved that this ordeal was over. I sat on his chest…and waited. Fortunately, someone—maybe the cabbie—had finally contacted the cops…I could hear the sound of sirens approaching.

Epilogue:

The police came, arrested the culprit, and took him away to be charged and sentenced. I wasn't required to make a court appearance but I know from subsequent newspaper clippings that—W.S.T. as he shall be known—received a 3-year sentence. He was a 33-year-old guy from Hamilton, of no fixed address, with a history of recent hold-ups and break-ins and subsequent jail time. The day prior to robbing the Herb and Spice Store, he'd held up Hillary Cleaners on Alta Vista. Although he didn't have a gun, he made the claim that he did while sticking his hand in his pocket and pointing it at Debbie, the cashier…this is considered armed robbery.

…and for my efforts? I received thanks and a small bag of produce from the owner…and a hug, and perhaps, a slight elevation of esteem in the eyes of Debbie T. I was, after all, her accidental hero.

All Roads at Any Time

11

The Coup d'Etat
"Apópse tha Pethánei o Fasismós!" (Tonight, Fascism will die!)

"Kathy and I are getting kinda low on cash so we're thinking of going to Israel to work on a Kibbutz...we get free room and board if we work on one of their farms...it's kinda like a commune or something."

It's Saturday, November 10, 1973, and I am in Athens with my two high school friends and travelling companions, Keith and Kathy, who've just decided to go to Israel, to extend their overseas trip, by exchanging labor for food and a bed. Our planned round-the-world trip together, has lasted barely 2 months, and we haven't even left Europe.

"That's kinda crazy," I said, "Israel just had a big war with all of her Arab neighbors barely two weeks ago. It's pretty dangerous there right now Keith, thousands were killed and you guys don't know what you're getting into."

I'm not sure if KandK's motivation was genuinely to save money, or if their foray into a war zone was driven by Kathy's desire to calve her malleable boyfriend Keith away from his high school chum—myself—so she could have more one-on-one quality time with her guy. If so, it seemed like a fairly extreme money-saving solution, or relationship building exercise. (I guess I could call them and ask, 50 years later, although they are no longer a couple, we are still friends.)

In any event, I chose not to join them, preferring instead "*to go to Istanbul*", according to my journal, and carry on with my global adventure.

They left without fanfare or delay and were gone the following day, Sunday the 11th, flying off into Armageddon as I remained in Athens, eighteen and alone.

According to a journal entry from that day though, their

departure left me somewhat nonplussed:

"Said goodbyes to Keith and Kathy, sorry to see them go but I think I'll get more accomplished now. Lazed around playing chess and cards"

...evidently my ideas of accomplishment lacked a certain get-ahead quality—even then!

I was staying at the "New Youth Hostel #4", at 3 Hamilton Street (now Chamilton), 97B Patision (now 28th Octovriou (October) Street) in Downtown Athens, just a few short blocks away from the Polytechnion (the National Technical University) where a student uprising would explode within the next few days, resulting in much death, destruction, and ultimately, the overthrow of dictator George Papadopolous.

I'm not sure if I should say that my days leading up to the revolution were blissfully unaware, or admit that they were pathetically uninformed.

I was completely oblivious to the political upheaval which was brewing in my neighbourhood. My fellow travellers seemed unconcerned, the Athenians with whom we interacted were not discussing it, and I was preoccupied with my travel plans, petty concerns and pleasures.

On Monday November 12, just three days before the students went on strike and occupied the Polytechnic, I was busy assembling the illegal documents I would need—primarily fake student I.D.—from a place called "Antonio's" in downtown Athens, to get discounts on my flight to Istanbul.

According to my Journal, I was much more concerned about:

Cold Showers: *"the energy shortage is giving us cold showers...what a drag"*

Eating: *"Went for food with Pearl and Dave"*

Drinking: *"Met some insane Australians"* (which probably meant that they drank more than me), and;

Playing: *"cards and chess"*

Eat Drink Play...the book.

And, perhaps the greatest example of my complete detachment from the political turmoil unfolding around me, my entry from Wednesday November 14—the first day of the student occupation:

Nov 14—Wednesday "When I don't write every day, I find I really forget what's happened anyway. It's kind of a drag, reading, sleeping, eating".

My self-indulgent ennui was about to change.

Student protest is not a new thing. Wikipedia lists 49 notable demonstrations going all the way back to the University of Paris Strike of 1229. My favourite being 'The Great Butter Rebellion' at Harvard in 1766…just for the name alone, "Mr. President we must do something about this Butter Rebellion…it's starting to spread!"

The late 1960s and early 70s were a time of much student unrest. 1968 was particularly tumultuous, with a worldwide escalation of, demonstrations, sit-ins, riots and revolutions taking place in well over 20 countries. These uprisings were mostly directed against military and bureaucratic elites, who countered with greater repression. This is exactly where Greek students of the Polytechnion found themselves in the fall of 1973.

Greeks had been chafing under the repressive regime of the military junta since 1967. Known as 'The Regime of the Colonels' or just 'The Dictatorship', leader Georgios Papadopolous, abolished civil rights, dissolved political parties, and exiled, imprisoned, and tortured politicians and citizens based on their political beliefs. An assassination attempt, in 1968, and a student self-immolation (Kostas Georgakis) in 1970 failed to change history.

Despite further repression, and American support for the Dictatorship, by late 1973, students in Athens were angry enough to make their move.

On November 14, 1973, while I was evidently dealing with the hardship of endless reading, eating, and sleeping, the students of the Polytechnion—blocks from my bed at Hostel #4—decided to take their lives in their hands and occupy the University.

On Thursday, November 15, the second day of the student occupation, thousands of citizens from Athens and the surrounding area, headed towards the Polytechnion to support the students. A radio transmitter had been set up on campus demanding the restoration of democracy—acting as a magnet for the disaffected.

Still unaware of the magnitude of events that were unfolding around me, I arose, ate breakfast and decided to wander up 28th Octovriou Street towards the American Express office where I was expecting some mail (in those days, Amex was one of the only ways to receive snail mail while overseas). Within a few blocks of the Hostel, it became apparent that "something was going on"—the streets became more and more crowded the closer I got to the University, traffic was down to a trickle or stopped altogether, and there was a sense of excitement and anticipation in the air.

My first journal reference goes thus, *"Watched a demonstration, very interesting, not enough leaders, publicity or organization…"*

My one experience, attending an anti-nuclear (Amchitka) demonstration in Victoria some years prior had evidently made me an expert, or at least a critic, qualified to provide such astute political commentary.

I do recall, on this day, being able to get fairly close to the barricaded gates of the Polytechnion. There were placards and protest signs stuck everywhere, while people milled around and the crowd swelled. I recall watching from the sidelines during the day, as different groups allied with the students started to arrive—third parties such as construction workers and farmers joined the demonstration, and at one point a large throng of "suits" showed up which were reputed to be bankers and businessmen.

By this point I had gleaned—through conversations with some English-speaking protesters—what the demonstration was about and what was at stake.

As a young, long-haired, left-of-centre traveller my sympathies were definitely with the students, but, as a non-resident just learning in real-time what was happening in front of me, I felt emotionally detached from the passions I was witnessing. I was a concerned spectator, a witness. It was fascinating and exciting, but I got hungry and I left, carrying on with my evening routine of exploration and the quest for food friends and fun.

I may have gone to the Plaka (entertainment district), perhaps I climbed up to the Acropolis or Filopappou Hill to watch the sunset, these details escape me and are not really germane to the story—I do know that my journey back to Hostel #4 at days end took me once again past the Polytechnion and what I am now referring to in my journal as "the riot".

"…went back to the riot… got talking to a bunch of students, took a couple of dangerous pictures."

Night time brings an edgy quality to the angry passions of young males. There was now a sense of lawlessness on the street as the government had not—as yet—decided to respond. Lots of clenched fists and mass chants of "Bread! Education! Freedom!", or, one which has stuck in my mind since that evening "Apópse tha pethánei o Fasismós!" (which, translates roughly, in English as, "Tonight Fascism will die!").

Maybe the uprising was going to work. Maybe the demands for justice, freedom, civil rights and democracy would prevail—or maybe American Vice-President Spiro Agnew would parachute naked into Syntagma Square spewing more pro-junta drivel like "the best thing to happen to Greece since Pericles ruled in ancient Athens"

I know, I know…the junta was installed at the height of the Cold War during America's fight against Communism. And Greece had fought a divisive Civil War, pitting left vs right in what is considered the first conflict of the Cold War. It's all so complex—but could be resolved so easily and amicably with the "Bathgate Solution." Better… *"leaders, publicity (and) organization."*

I edged my way into the crowds of protesters and decided I would take a picture with my shitty little 1970s Kodak Pocket Instamatic Camera and its weird little flash attachment.

I stood out like a sore thumb with my long strawberry-blond hair, patched jeans, foreign culture coat, and large caulk boots (with their spikes removed—a remnant of my brief career as a tree-spacer with Macmillan Bloedel.)

When the protesters saw that I was a foreigner with a camera they encouraged their fellow insurrectionists to sit on the street, so I could get a better shot of their protest (this was only a fraction of what was going on) and tell the world what was happening in their country.

At the same time, I was told that what I was doing was dangerous and that there were secret police keeping an eye on the protesters and would not think kindly of someone recording it, and even worse, being mistaken for an American.

From the Journal: *"got asked if I was American—<u>never</u> say yes (even if you are)".*

Given American support for this unpopular regime, and considering where I was standing this was definitely not an auspicious time and place to admit to being American. I flashed the Canadian flag sewn onto my day satchel and apologized—to prove I was Canadian—and escaped the wrath of the mob.

Friday November 16. Morning arrived, the uprising had not yet coalesced into revolution, and Papadopolous was still in power.

For we hostelers there was really nothing to do but go about our day. None of us knew what the final outcome would be, although it seemed likely that there could only be one of two possible outcomes—the students would prevail and democracy would be restored, or they would be crushed and the regime would cling to power. The final outcome would prove to be much more Machiavellian in the complex calculus of Dictatorships and great power politics.

Despite being less than a kilometer from the uprising, Hostel #4 was still a place of relative calm. This could not be said of the rest of Athens. Sometime during the day, a proclamation was announced that the students intended to bring down the junta. Demonstrations and attacks against neighboring ministries took place, central roads were closed, fires erupted and Molotov cocktails were thrown in Athens for the first time.

The Junta decided to reply firmly, and repress the rebellion. Battle lines were drawn.

As evening descended, I met two friends—Betty and Anne—from a nearby hostel who wanted to walk to the Plaka for dinner. A little Moussaka, Retsina and music sounded good. It was Friday night after all and, thus far, we had not witnessed or experienced anything that gave us pause in our normal activities. The most direct route would take us—once again—past the Polytechnion, ground zero of the revolution.

There was little or no automobile traffic so we were able to walk on the streets on our way to Omonia Square, enroute to the Plaka. Crowds of Athenians, students and otherwise, milled about. There was garbage in the streets as one might find after a parade or festival. As foreigners we were certainly being observed but no one seemed hostile and there was—at this point—no government presence. No police or military in sight. This was soon to change.

We got to Omonia without incident and veered left onto Stadiou on our way to Syntagma Square which is a few short blocks from the Plaka. Suddenly, halfway up Satadiou Street, people on the sidewalk ahead of us, turned and started running towards us. Pursuing them, was a phalanx of policemen with clubs, charging down the street, beating pedestrians indiscriminately. We could see their clubs rising and falling of the backs and heads of those that were fleeing towards us.

It took a moment to fully grasp what was going. Moments before the mayhem reached us, I grabbed Betty and Anne and pulled them into a store hoping to avoid being clubbed or run over by fleeing pedestrians. One of the young policemen, rushed into the store after us wielding a club over his head as if to strike, screamed something unintelligible, as we cowered on the floor, then abruptly, turned and left and ran to re-join his comrades.

We gathered ourselves and exited the store to find broken windows and people clutching their bruised and bloodied heads, while some tended to the injured.

We were all shaken by this new, violent display. Not wanting to follow in the same direction the police had taken, we carried on with our original plan to head to the Plaka, find a taverna, have a drink, and gain insight into what was going on. No more leisurely Friday night stroll. People ran furtively to their altered destinations or gathered on street corners deep in conversation while casting fearful glances. It was around this time that we began to hear the first gunshots echoing in the distance.

"Tonight, is the night of the Revolution," said Dmitri, owner of the little Taverna that we liked to frequent.

"I suggest you return to your Hostel… it is going to get too dangerous on the streets for you. The police are out now beating people and taking some away." "We think Papadopolous will send in the military…already there is shooting but we don't know who is shooting who."

"How should we get back?" I asked, "the Polytechnion is directly between us and our Hostel?".

"Don't go back the way you came," he said, "you will have to make a big detour."

We headed out, unsure of our route, but knowing that we had to give the University a wide berth. It seemed wise to avoid major routes so we chose a series of narrow streets which hugged the slopes of Lycabettus Hill. We headed roughly northeast to avoid the turmoil, asking people for directions and guidance as we went.

It's about 11pm now and gunfire, including automatic fire was being heard more frequently. Apparently, the regime had sent snipers into the city near the Polytechnion to assassinate students. We were running into other people who were fleeing the conflict—some of which were suffering from tear gas exposure.

"Here is some vaseline for your eyes," said one Athenian we encountered, "it will protect you from the tear gas."

We applied it as directed, and carried on.

Betty and Anne were staying at a different Hostel than myself, several blocks farther away from the University, so I decided to get them home safely before I returned to #4. After what seemed like an extremely long, arduous and nerve-wracking detour through the side streets and back alleys of Athens we arrived—safely—at their Hostel, hugged and said our goodbyes.

From here it seemed worth the risk to take the main road—Patision (28th Octovriou)—back to Hostel #4.

It is now Saturday the 17th around 1am. Patision was unrecognizable. City transit buses had been hijacked and overturned all along the main drag, acting—I imagine—as barriers to the anticipated military assault and as protection against police attacks which were now ongoing. Students would run from behind overturned buses to hurl rocks and Molotov cocktails, and then retreat to the relative safety of the barricade. Often it was not enough, as small groups of police would corner a student (or a citizen) and beat them mercilessly and then drag them off to awaiting police vans.

My route back to Hostel #4 was not far, but it was an obstacle course of broken glass, small fires, and trying to avoid the wrath of the police. By the time I got back to the Hostel most of the other inhabitants had returned and were either sitting together in the common areas with worried, fearful looks, or had ascended to the roof for a better view of the mayhem on the streets below.

I decided to join the rooftop crowd.

There were around ten or fifteen of us on the slippery red-tile roof, clinging to our positions so we could witness the fight between the protesters and the police—and avoid plunging to the street below. One fellow had a professional-looking Nikon camera and was taking night photos which required no flash, whereas I, with my cheap Kodak Pocket Instamatic decided to try my hand at a night shot using my flash at perhaps two or three hundred feet…which gives very poor results.

I don't know if my flash alerted the sniper to our presence, but within minutes a hail of bullets passed within inches of our heads. I could have reached up and caught one.

Everybody let out a collective "FUCK!" and rolled, slithered and crawled—as fast as was humanely possible—off the roof and back into the relative safety of the Hostel. Some of the women were in tears, and everybody was agitated, fearful, and excited. No one knew if the sniper missed intentionally, or, if we had just "dodged a bullet". Either way, the adrenaline was pumping, it was 2 or 3 in the morning, and sleep was not an option.

And then the military moved in.

I remember hearing the distant rumble. The tanks and military vehicles coming down Patision Street were audible from many, many blocks away. I and several others made our way to the second-floor balcony on Chamilton Street where we had a good view of Patision to see what was in store for the protesters. Within minutes a giant rumbling AMX-30 tank came into view heading towards the Polytechnion.

Whichever buses and cars the tank could not push aside with its massive weight and bulk it drove over and crushed. On top of each tank was a soldier with a pivoting machine gun, firing indiscriminately. Big chunks of plaster flung of the buildings across from us as the bullets pinged and whizzed.

From my journal: "*Saturday November 17– "Late at night most people are awake (early Saturday) the sound of guns is so loud and close it's deafening."*

The tank carried on down 28th Octovriou, making its way inexorably to the gates of the Polytechnion. Once there, it turned to face the University and the gates and drove directly through and over the main steel entrance to the campus, to which people were clinging.

At this point, Spyros Markezinis (Greece's Prime Minister— briefly) had to request that Papadopoulos reimpose martial law. A radio station had been constructed on campus (using laboratory equipment) which repeatedly implored Athenians to join their struggle. As the military enters the campus a young man's voice could be heard desperately asking the soldiers (whom he calls 'brothers in arms') surrounding the building complex to disobey the military orders and not to fight 'brothers protesting'. The voice carries on to an emotional pitch, reciting the lyrics of the Greek National Anthem, until the tank enters the yard, at which time transmission ceases.

The uprising has been crushed.

There are some disputes over the size of the military operation and the number of people killed. Wikipedia notes: "An "official investigation" ... "recorded casualties amount(ing) to 24 civilians killed outside Athens Polytechnic campus" The records of the trials held following the collapse of the Junta document the circumstances of the "deaths of many civilians during the uprising". The Athenians I spoke with said that up to 200 had been killed.

From the Journal:

"Daytime. The tanks and armoured cars arrived today, it's a real freak-out. The papers say 4 dead the people say 200...who knows? Not us, I wouldn't walk out in the streets to look. Started work today, 50 drachmas and a bed, the manager is a real ass, he pinches pennies and is never satisfied...

Fifty Drachmas and a bed for janitorial work at the hostel. I left this tidbit in as a nod to how rapidly life returns to the commonplace. Soldiers are still shooting at people blocks from where I am, yet toilets still need to be cleaned, beds made and floors washed, and I'm angry with my cheap manager. Atrocities are being committed, tragedy is unfolding, yet interpersonal exchanges still provide fodder for comedy—would you like some more pita with your tzatziki?

"Today they started curfew after 4 o'clock, no food til Monday so we shop now. Prices raised, streets deserted, some windows smashed. Came back to tear gas after breakfast, one guy showed us two kinds of bombs (tear gas) that he found, both American makes...Tonight the streets are dead. No action, scattered shots with occasional machine gun bursts. Some people got stuck across town after curfew—tough luck."

In the days following the military clampdown it looked like the Junta had won. The rebels had been killed, injured, captured or had fled. The rest of the city was on edge and we were all subject to a 7:00 p.m. curfew. I was still trying to arrange passage to Istanbul in this new restrictive environment.

"It's scary downtown, at 6 the people are all hurrying home...Just made it but I can't get comfortable here"...

And then, on November 25th, the day before I was scheduled to fly to Istanbul, in what seemed—at that time—to be sweet poetic justice, Colonel Georgios Papadopolous, the Dictator, was overthrown in a coup d'etat.

On the surface, to an outsider like myself, it appeared to be cause for celebration—the student's sacrifices had not been in vain, their efforts had indeed led to the fall of this repressive regime. The truth, as it turned out, was much more complex and would take many twists and turns over the next seven months. I couldn't stay to find out—I flew to Istanbul the next morning.

Denouement

One critical piece of this story—which was not revealed to me for many years—was that Papadopolous had actually been attempting to liberalize the regime in the late 60's and early 70's prior to the student uprising.

Many restrictions had been lifted and the army's role significantly reduced. His attempts at "gradual democratization" had failed, however, and hardliners within the military were looking for a pretext to return the country to a more "orthodox" military dictatorship. The student uprising gave Brigadier Dimitrios Ioannidis a casus belli to oust Papadopolous, and replace him as the new strongman of the regime. Thus, the student revolt had an opposite effect—it led to even more repression and further suspension of rights and freedoms.

But all was not lost! In the Machiavellian labyrinth of Greek Politics, Ioannidis made a fatal miscalculation by staging an abortive coup against Archbishop Makarios—the President of Cyprus—in July 1974. This resulted in an invasion of Cyprus by Turkey which subsequently caused the military regime to implode. These events ushered in the era of metapoltefsi (Greek for "polity/regime change). Parliamentary democracy was restored, and the elections of 1974 were the first free elections held in a decade.

And Keith and Kathy?... in their Israeli kibbutz in a war zone? They stayed several months and passed their time in peace and harmony—L'Chaim!

All Roads at Any Time

12

"No Room at the Café"—A Christmas Story

It was the last few minutes, of the last day, of the final weekend of my Fall/Winter season, before I closed up Shavasana Gallery and Café for the year.

On this particular day—unlike all the others—I was shutting down an hour early, at three o'clock, to give myself enough time to do a detailed cleaning of the Gallery in anticipation of hosting my family there the following weekend, for Christmas dinner. It was Sunday, December 18th, the first day of Hanukkah, exactly a week before Christmas, and I could see a light snow falling through the steamy single pane windows. The few customers I had left were fine with an earlier closing, except for my neighbour Billie who had just sat down to a plate of cookies and a Brown Betty teapot full of English Breakfast and Mint.

"Don't worry Billie," I said, "I see that you've got a full pot of tea there, why don't you just hang out while I do some cleaning".

After all, it was "Island Time", the loose rules and flexible schedules that seem to govern any notion of time on the Gulf Islands. Billie could sip and nibble and chat while I dusted, swept and mopped. I brought in my roadside sandwich board, and my Easel Signage, and put up my "Closed" sign to dissuade any latecomers.

As the light began to wane, and the flurry of snow gathered pace, Billie noticed, out of the corner of her eye, a couple walking towards the front door and said,

"Oh oh…here come some people, I'll tell them you're closed."

She got off her chair, opened the door and said,

"Sorry, the café is closed for the day."

I couldn't see who it was outside but I could almost feel their dismay at being turned away. There was likely very little else open at that time of day on a Sunday in December. Realizing that I still had a supply of hot coffee in the Zojirushi, and lots of hot water on hand for tea, and the ever-present supply of cookies, I said,

"Hang on there a sec Billie, maybe they'd like a hot beverage to go"

I went to the door and greeted a 30-ish couple—dusted in snow—and invited them in, explaining that I was indeed closing down but could set them up with a hot coffee or tea—if they liked.

Thrilled to be invited into a warm space with the prospect of a hot drink, they joined us inside, expressing thanks and gratitude for not having been turned away. They had no car and—despite the weather—were on a walking adventure around Mayne Island, cherishing a chance to get away from the city and unwind a bit. I would soon find out how far they had come to unwind.

Shavasana Gallery was the third place they'd gone that was either closed or shutting down—an unfamiliar experience for a young urban couple having their first foray to a Gulf Island. As I prepared a couple of hot chocolates for them, Billie decided to pay up and go so I wished her a Merry Christmas and gave her a little hug as I was unlikely to see her when I returned the following week.

While I stirred their hot chocolates and chatted with them about a myriad of things, I could detect accents that I was unable to place, so, as is my nature I asked where they were from.

"Kazakhstan", replied the young woman, "And Ukraine", replied the young man.

"Wow", I said, slightly surprised, "I don't think I've ever met anyone from Kazakhstan, very nice to meet you." "And Ukraine…," I said, momentarily at an, uncharacteristic, loss for words.

Although I have known Ukrainians, and had Canadians of Ukrainian descent as friends all my life, I don't think I have been in the presence of a Ukrainian since the horrible invasion of their country began earlier this year. All that I could do was place my hand over my heart and express my profound sympathy, support and compassion for the suffering that he and his fellow Ukrainians have been going through.

"I'm so sorry for what has been happening to Ukraine since the invasion" I said, "how are you doing?" "I am doing OK thanks", he said, "I've been in Canada for a while now, and have recently managed to bring my family over—so for this I am happy" he said, smiling.

I can only try and imagine his relief.

"Even though Mayne Island is far away from the war in Ukraine," I said, "the people here do care and try and help where we can."

I drew his attention to a book by Julie Emerson which I had on display for sale on the main table.

"Julie created this book of stories and illustrations—all about Ukraine—and we are donating 100% of the sales to Ukraine Relief efforts."

He picked up a copy and flipped through it, admiring Julie's work.

"And another one of my artists, Famous Empty Sky, donated 10% of all sales of her art to Ukraine Relief …I think we raised several hundred dollars."

"That is wonderful," he said, "every little bit helps…"

As I was handing them their hot chocolates and preparing to send them on their way—back out into the snow and gathering dusk—I found myself hit by a case of "the feels".

"Can I give you a hug?" I asked, "Yes, of course," he said, smiling, arms outstretched. As we embraced, his lovely Kazakhstani wife—smiling broadly—opened her arms and said, "Me too!"

As a hugger, it doesn't take much convincing for me to hug everyone in a room. I gave her a big hug, shook both their hands and wished them all the best for a peaceful, gentler 2023….and said goodbye.

Here's hoping and praying, that all of our wishes for Peace in Ukraine come true soon.

All Roads at Any Time

ABOUT THE AUTHOR

A creative generalist who continues to surf new and familiar waves of expression through art, music and writing, George Bathgate, is the Co-Creator/Artistic Director/Writer for experimental theatre group, Just Push Play Audiomotion Theatre. He is also currently Curator/Proprietor of Shavasana Art Gallery and Café, on Mayne Island, where he exhibits local art, makes a pretty good Latté, creates ceramic masks, and Writes/Blogs about these experiences—and more—on two of his websites: shavasana.ca and clayandbone.com During the pandemic he launched a podcast—The Accidental Curator—theaccidentalcurator.ca which has become a new medium for writing, narration, and interviews. He has been told he has a great 'radio face.'

George divides his time between his home in Kitsilano, and Mayne Island where his Gallery Café is located.

Manufactured by Amazon.ca
Bolton, ON

39239881R00061